PLENTY OF L⌣⌣⌣

Plenty, FL 3

Lara Valentine

MENAGE EVERLASTING

Siren Publishing, Inc.
www.SirenPublishing.com

A SIREN PUBLISHING BOOK
IMPRINT: Ménage Everlasting

PLENTY OF LOVE
Copyright © 2013 by Lara Valentine

ISBN: 978-1-62242-380-4

First Printing: February 2013

Cover design by Les Byerley
All art and logo copyright © 2013 by Siren Publishing, Inc.

PUBLISHER
Siren Publishing, Inc.
www.SirenPublishing.com

DEDICATION

To all of us who wish Plenty, Florida, was real.

PLENTY OF LOVE

Plenty, FL 3

LARA VALENTINE

Chapter 1

"You're a treasure, Becca. You really are."

Becca smiled at Addie, the elderly woman she had been bringing a hot meal two days a week for the last four months. She was a volunteer for the meals program Dr. Steve had started to assist patients who had undergone serious surgery and long rehabilitations.

"You're a treasure, too, Addie. I hope you like chicken and broccoli. It looks really good today."

Becca pulled the foil-covered tray from the cooler and set it on the kitchen table. Although Addie had joined the program when a broken hip had impeded her ability to care for herself, she still liked to sit at the table and eat what she called a "civilized meal." Becca always delivered to Addie last so she could sit and hear Addie's stories of Plenty's past. Addie was an avid storyteller, and Becca was her biggest fan.

"I do not like broccoli, but at my age you eat what is good for you. I'll have gas all afternoon, thank you very much. Good thing I live alone."

Becca smothered a giggle at Addie's plain speech. She decided to change the subject. "What story are you going to tell me today? Last time we talked about the repressive fifties in Plenty."

Addie bit into the steamed broccoli and pulled a face of distaste. "I'm not going to tell any stories today, young lady. You are going to tell me about the upcoming wedding."

Addie's blue-gray eyes got misty and far away. "I've always loved weddings. Plenty has seen some real doozies, too." Addie shook her head and returned to the present. "But none I'm going to tell you about today. So when do you leave for Key West? It would be nice just to get out of the house now and then. You're lucky."

Becca's father and his partner were marrying in Key West. They were not marrying each other. They were marrying Ellie Miller, recently from Chicago, Illinois. Ellie had come to Plenty over the holidays to visit her daughter and Becca's friend, Jillian Miller. Ellie, Mike Parks, who was Becca's father, and Steve had quickly fallen in love and started planning a wedding. To make matters more interesting, Ellie's daughter Jillian had fallen in love with Becca's two brothers, Sheriff Ryan Parks and firefighter Jackson Parks. They were all about to become one big, happy family.

"I leave in a week. I'm driving down with Jillian, Ryan, and Jackson. Cassie and her men will be right behind us in the motorcade. Leading the way will be Ellie, Dad, and Steve. I'm looking forward to getting away for more than a few days. I haven't taken a vacation in over a year. Well, a real one anyway. I can get out of the salon for a day or two here and there, but it's hard to get away for an extended time."

Cassie and Jillian had moved to Plenty last summer to start new lives. They had certainly succeeded. Cassie, the former accountant, now taught math at the town school and was engaged to Zach and Chase Harper, local businessmen. Jillian, the former attorney, now taught history and was engaged to Ryan and Jack. Becca envied her friends. They had found their true loves. Ménage loves. Plenty, Florida, was a ménageamous town. The town was tolerant of alternative lifestyles, and polyamory was no exception.

Addie sighed. "Dr. Steve said I can start walking in my garden soon. I've missed my walks. Having the physical therapist come to my house just isn't the same."

Becca smiled in sympathy. Addie was used to being more active. She liked to garden and walk into town and have tea at the diner. She hadn't been able to do that for months.

"You'll be up and around in no time. Dr. Steve is the best doctor in Plenty."

"He'll have company soon, won't he? Isn't your friend's brother moving to town soon to join Dr. Steve's practice?"

Becca nodded. "Dr. Mark Miller will be joining Dr. Steve's practice. It will be good to have another doctor in town. We need one."

Addie gave her a shrewd look. "Didn't you spend quite a bit of time with Dr. Miller when he was visiting at Thanksgiving and Christmas?"

Becca's thoughts drifted to Dr. Mark Miller, Jillian's brother and a talented doctor from Chicago. He and his attorney husband, Travis Andrews, would be moving to Plenty in a few weeks. Both Mark and Travis were gorgeous and sexy. They were also totally taken—with each other. Becca simply had to stop fantasizing about the two of them. It was hard to stop. They were wonderful men that she had gotten to know when they visited at Thanksgiving and then again for a few weeks at Christmas. Each moment she spent with them only made her want to spend more time with them.

"I guess I did. I spend a lot of time with Cassie and Jillian, so it was only natural to spend time with Jillian's brother and his husband. They're very nice men."

And good looking, too.

"I assume they'll be at the wedding?"

"Yes, the whole family plus Zach and Chase with Cassie, of course."

"Is Josh going with you?"

Becca bit her lip and considered how to answer the question. She had dated Josh Kent, the owner of Plenty's one and only coffee shop, a few times. So far, it had been light and casual, although she suspected that Josh was more serious about her than she was about him. There was just no zing with Josh. He was gorgeous enough, smart, and very sweet. Why she had to spend her time drooling over Mark and Travis she had no idea. They were no better looking than Josh, really.

Okay, maybe a little better looking in her opinion. Mark looked like a surfer god with his blond hair, steely blue eyes, and broad shoulders. Travis was the brooding hunk with his brown hair, chocolate-brown eyes, and muscled arms. Whenever she thought of them, her body responded with a wet pussy and tight nipples. Her pulse was racing just picturing them.

"No, he has to stay and run the coffee shop. His silent partners haven't arrived in Plenty yet. They're still in New York. I'll be all on my own. A single girl on the prowl."

Addie snorted. "I can't say that Key West is a great place for a single girl to find a man. It seems like you could use one, Becca. It's not good for a young woman to be alone."

Becca couldn't agree more.

"I'm fine. I'll find the right man one day." *Or maybe two.*

"You have to look to find. Is Josh the one?"

Becca opened her mouth to say maybe then shut it in defeat. She shook her head. "No, he's not. I wish he was, but he's not."

"Best tell him and move on then. It's not fair to keep him thinking it could be something."

"No, it's not. But who do I move on to then? I know every man in this town. And it ain't happening with any of them."

"The Lord will provide. Until then, be on the lookout. The right man could show up at any moment."

"Hellooo! Addie! Helloo!"

Addie smiled and waved as a man around Becca's own age walked through the door. He wasn't very tall but could be called handsome in a pretty-boy sort of way.

"Randall, I'm surprised to see you today. I want you to meet my friend, Becca. Becca, this is my grandnephew, Randall. I've told you about him."

Becca knew Randall was a successful real estate developer in Orlando and the grandson of Addie's deceased sister. Becca had also heard Randall was something of a ladies' man. *Ick.* He definitely was not her type.

"I came to see my favorite great-aunt. Can't a man be spontaneous? I brought you some of those cupcakes you like from the bakery near my house."

Randall leaned down and kissed Addie's cheek before turning to shake Becca's hand. Becca's skin crawled a little as he looked her up and down like he was appraising a painting. She pulled her hand away.

"It's nice to meet you, Randall."

Randall must have decided he liked what he saw. He gave her a slippery smile. "Please, call me...Randy."

Ewww.

"Well, I need to be going, Addie, Randall. I need to get back to the shop."

Becca owned the only hair salon in Plenty. That was why she hadn't had a real vacation in over a year.

"Randy, please. I hope we meet again."

Becca suppressed a shudder. There was something really creepy about this guy. She had good instincts about people, and Randall was someone she needed to stay away from.

Randall plopped down into the chair she had just vacated. "Now, Auntie, we need to talk about the investment opportunity again. I'm worried you'll outlive your money. This investment is a sure thing."

Becca knew there was no such thing but was too polite to say. She thought about lingering to hear what he was trying to talk her into, but it was really none of her business. She quickly gathered the cooler and headed for the front door, waving a cheerful good-bye to Addie. There was something not quite right about that man.

* * * *

Becca pushed open the door of Josh's Java. Addie was right. She needed to talk to Josh and tell him there was no chance the relationship was going to move forward. He was a nice guy and didn't deserve to be led on.

It was the middle of the afternoon and the shop wasn't busy. Just a few customers sat near the back sipping coffee and staring at their laptops. She waved at Josh. He turned and gave her a big smile, his hand on another man's shoulder. It was then she noticed the two men leaning against the counter. She had never seen them before, but Josh's relaxed body language signaled they were friends.

Josh leaned down and lightly kissed her cheek. "Hey, I didn't expect to see you this afternoon. I'm glad you're here, though. I want you to meet my friends."

Becca turned to introduce herself and was immediately taken aback. The tallest man, he must have been about six three or four, looked pale and haggard, as if he was just recovering from a nasty flu. Despite his pallor, she could see he was usually quite handsome, his jaw strong and his profile sharp. His eyes were shadowed. His head was shaved. He had wide shoulders, although his clothes hung on his large frame. Yes, this man had recently been ill.

The second man, on the other hand, looked like he had just stepped from the cover of *GQ*. Golden-brown hair was pulled back into a ponytail, which only highlighted his classically handsome face. He wore an impeccable blue suit, which looked incongruous in the casual atmosphere.

The right man could show up at any moment.

She looked at him and felt…nothing. Absolutely nothing.

"This is Brayden Tyler"—Josh indicated the taller man—"and Falk O'Neill." He pointed to the male-model guy. "They're my best friends since college days and my silent partners. They're finally moving here from New York."

Becca shook hands with each of them before turning to Josh. "I really need to talk to you, but maybe I should come back."

"Of course not, I can talk to you now. The guys need to head to the house and start unpacking anyway. Right?"

The men reluctantly pushed away from the counter and headed for the door, bidding them both good-bye.

"Let's go back to my office. Tommy can handle the counter."

Josh led her back to his office and indicated she should sit while he sat opposite her. She plucked up her courage. This wouldn't be easy. Josh gave her a gentle smile.

"Actually, I wanted to talk to you, too, Becca. You came at the perfect moment."

"You did? Well, you go ahead then." She wasn't in any hurry to hurt Josh's feelings.

"What did you think of Brayden and Falk?"

"Um, I don't really know. I just met them. Why?"

Josh had a serious expression. "They're my best friends. We didn't pick this town randomly. We came here because of its reputation for tolerating ménage relationships. That's what the three of us want."

Josh's words finally sunk in. "The three of you…with me? Is that what you're asking?"

Josh nodded, his words careful. "Yes. I've been telling them about you. They were excited to meet you. Did you like them?"

Becca closed her eyes for a moment, knowing this was going to go badly. "I liked them fine. But…"

Josh's lips twisted. "But?"

Becca sat back in the chair. "I came here to tell you that I don't think this relationship is going to work out. I like you, but…well…there's no…spark, you know what I mean? I'm so sorry. I really am."

Becca felt terrible, but Josh captured her hand in his. "It's okay. I think you're wonderful, Becca. Sweet and pretty, and kind. I know we've only been out on a few dates, and here I've sprung two friends on you. It's not like we've had sex, either. I'm disappointed, I admit it, but you're probably right. I've never been in love before, so I wouldn't recognize it if it happened."

Becca's heart squeezed as she thought of Mark and Travis. They were the type of men she could fall in love with given some encouragement. She wouldn't get any encouragement, of course. But she could still let them star in her late-night fantasies.

"I've never been in love before, either. But from what I've seen you'll recognize it when it happens. Love smacks you upside the head and throws you to the ground. If you don't feel that way about me, then you're not in love with me. I've seen it enough to know."

Josh laughed. "Shit, that just sounds painful. How about this? How about we stay friends? I like you, and I like spending time with you. No getting smacked in the head allowed."

Becca relaxed a little. It appeared Josh hadn't felt any more zing than she had. "I heartily agree to your suggestion. No one wants to get smacked in the head."

Josh's expression suddenly turned concerned. "Hell. I'm so stupid when it comes to women. You want to be in love like that, don't you? Do you have any candidate in mind?"

"No, of course not! It's just…oh, never mind."

Josh gave her an encouraging smile. "Do you want me to try and make him jealous? I'd be happy to. It sounds like fun. Of course, if he can't see how wonderful you are for himself, then he probably doesn't deserve you."

Becca could only close her eyes and think of Mark and Travis. Mark and Travis...the couple. They were so happy together. Their love for each other radiated from them. "You're right. Idiots. I'm much better without them. Now how about a latte?"

Josh gave her an appraising look. "Them, huh? I was right, wasn't I? You're a ménage type."

Becca felt her face get warm. "I've never...Okay, I'm the ménage type. Don't feel obliged to alert the media."

Josh chuckled. "Your secret is safe with me. Let's get you that latte—with a drop of something stronger. I don't know about you, but I could use it."

Becca knew it would take more than a coffee and a shot to get over her embarrassing crush on Mark and Travis. She would see them in a week at the wedding and was going to have to play it cool around them. It wouldn't be easy. Every time she saw them, she fell harder for them. She was just going to have to find another man and avoid Mark and Travis as much as possible.

Chapter 2

Mark sat at the granite island in the kitchen he'd shared with Travis Andrews for the last ten years surrounded by moving boxes. He and Travis had worked hard at decorating the palatial high-rise condo to create the home they had envisioned. Somehow it had never quite worked. They finally realized the condo didn't lack a new painting or a comfortable sofa. It lacked the warm, loving presence of a woman.

They hadn't been actively looking. They had given up on finding anyone. They loved each other and were happy with each other and the life they'd built. But their recent trips to Plenty had put thoughts of a woman front and center in their minds. One woman in particular—Becca Parks. They were both smitten. They had spent quite a bit of time with her on their two visits to Plenty and they were convinced she might be the woman they had given up on finding.

Becca was feisty and funny. She challenged them and wasn't impressed by their high-flying careers and money in Chicago. In fact, she seemed quite unimpressed. She judged people by how they cared for others, not their title or bank account. Mark remembered one particular conversation at Thanksgiving when Becca had asked Travis about the pro bono work he did for battered women. She hadn't asked about Travis's law partnership, his high-profile clients. She'd asked about his charity work. The way she looked at life and people made her even more attractive than her dainty blonde beauty.

And she was beautiful. But it took a back seat to who she was as a person. Mark and Travis were looking forward to getting to know her much better in the coming months. They wanted to see if perhaps this relationship between the three of them might really work.

Whenever they were with Becca, she seemed interested in them. Her body language told the story. She was attracted to them and they to her. They just wanted a chance to see if the relationship could go anywhere.

Mark rolled up a glass in packing paper and placed it carefully in the cushioned box before starting all over again with the next glass. Packing up a home they had lived in for the last ten years really sucked. It seemed like he and Travis had done nothing but buy crap for the last decade. They needed to do some serious purging before they moved to Plenty. That's what this move was about. They wanted to simplify their lives.

They had been talking about this for the last five years. Their lives had become one thing—work. They rarely had time for each other. It was when they were in Plenty that they rediscovered fun and their relationship. When they returned to Chicago, they looked around their condo and knew what they had to do.

The fact that they could get to know Becca was a major bonus, but they would have made the move anyway. She was the icing on the cake, so to speak. Mark hoped their instincts would prove to be correct. Finding someone they both liked and were attracted to had turned out to be impossible until Becca. And she had no idea how attractive they found her.

She was blonde, blue eyed, curvy, and a total sweetheart. She had charmed them from the first moment they had seen her picture. Jillian had e-mailed them a picture of herself, her friend Cassie, and Becca in their Halloween costumes. Becca had been dressed as a naughty nurse. Mark had since fantasized about spanking her for various behavior infractions. His dick was getting hard just thinking about it.

A warm male body pressed into his back. "Hmmm…you have quite the look on your face. What dirty thoughts lurk in the mind of my husband?"

Mark and Travis weren't legally married but had spoken vows to one another on the spur of the moment during a very romantic vacation in Hawaii. They were married in their hearts, if not in the state of Illinois.

"I was just remembering Becca in the nurse outfit. Do you think we can convince her to wear it again and play doctor?"

"Maybe we should start by convincing her to take a chance on an old married couple, babe. Jillian said that Becca has dated Josh a few times. You know, the guy who owns the coffee shop?"

Mark remembered him. Josh was handsome and charming. *Fuck.*

"I remember him. He's no competition. You're way sexier."

Travis stepped back and did a bump and grind with his hips. "I'm sexy and I know it. I think you're pretty fucking sexy, too. Especially when your sexy mouth is sucking my cock."

Mark laughed. "Is that a hint? Not very subtle."

"I'm not trying to be. Seems like we don't get to fuck very often these days. Always working. Oh wait, that's why we're moving to Plenty. To work less and fuck more."

"Seriously, Trav. You don't think Becca is serious about this Josh guy, do you?"

"Jillian said they weren't serious, babe. We have to believe her."

"We need to get moved and get down there before someone realizes how wonderful she is and steals her right from under our noses."

"You really want her, huh?"

Mark stiffened. "Don't you? I thought you were attracted to her, too. We both have to be for this. I don't want to screw up what we have. I love you."

"I am attracted to her. But you know me, babe. I'm a lot more cautious. We got to know her pretty well when we visited Plenty, but we need to spend more time with her. We need to court her."

"I know that. We need to get to know her, date her. But I'm hopeful, aren't you? We've wanted a woman to complete us. Becca's the first one we've agreed on."

They'd slept with women together before but never found a woman they would consider spending more than a weekend with. Becca was different. She wasn't a fling kind of girl. She was the real-thing kind of girl.

"I'm hopeful. But I'm also realistic. What are the chances she can love both of us and both of us love her? That's a tall order. Don't get me wrong, babe. I want this as much as you do. There are so many happy ménages in Plenty. I want us to be one of them. I'm just being cautious. The statistics aren't on our side."

"I know the numbers aren't on our side, but the numbers have never seen Becca. You're such a doubter. You need to believe, Trav. It's going to happen for us."

"I do believe, babe. I believe Becca might be the one. I believe time with her will tell us what we need to know."

Travis was a cautious, thoughtful man. It made him an amazing attorney who lost very few cases. His caution was also one of the things Mark loved about him and one of the things that made Mark crazy. Travis balanced Mark's gung-ho, grab-life-by-the-balls personality perfectly.

"I believe this move is good for us, Trav. You're becoming a cautious old man. You need to have a little carpe diem in your soul."

Travis grabbed the next glass and began helping Mark pack. "I have carpe diem. Just the other day, I decided to not call an opposing council when he expected me to. It made him sweat blood. By the time he called me, he was putty in my hands."

Mark rolled his eyes. "First thing we do when we get to Plenty is ask Ryan Parks to take us skydiving. You need to take a freakin' chance once in a while."

Travis laughed, but Mark was serious. He and Travis needed to take a chance on Becca Parks. If they didn't, they would always wonder if they had passed on a woman who would complete them.

* * * *

Becca parked her car in Ryan and Jack's driveway and dragged her suitcase behind her as she headed to Jillian's car. Ryan's SUV was in the shop, so they were driving Jillian's sensible four-door Honda Accord. Jack was making a fuss that they couldn't take his pickup truck. It was a double cab, so it had plenty of room, but the truck bed wasn't covered for their luggage.

"The luggage will be okay, Ryan. We can take my truck."

Ryan barely glanced at Jack. "It's supposed to rain. If Jillian's suitcase gets wet, along with her maid-of-honor dress, she'll kick your ass and mine, plus we'll be in the doghouse again. Fuck, we just got out. I'm not climbing in again because you don't like sedans. Suck it up, little brother."

Jack snorted but then smiled when he caught sight of Becca. "Hey, little sis. Ready to go?"

"I think so. Where's Jillian?"

Ryan pointed to the next car. Becca caught her breath as she realized it was Mark and Travis. She hadn't seen them since the week after Christmas. She was taken aback again at just how handsome they were. It looked like Travis was wearing his hair shorter, and Mark had grown a goatee, but they still looked basically the same. Devastating.

Jillian saw her and waved excitedly. "Hey, look who's moved here! Mark and Travis got in last night."

Becca walked toward them as if pulled by a magnet. She couldn't have walked away if her life depended on it. "Welcome to Plenty, guys. Did you have a good trip down?"

She congratulated herself on sounding casual and nonchalant.

Both men's faces split into grins, and she couldn't stop herself from returning their smile. She really was happy to see them.

Mark wrapped her in a bear hug. She breathed in his masculine scent, his muscles hard under her hands as she hugged him back.

"Missed you, pretty girl. Did you miss us?"

She felt his warm breath as he whispered in her ear. She felt a zing of electricity shoot up her spine and down to her pussy. Before she could answer, Travis was tugging her away from Mark for his own hug. His scent was just as tantalizing but slightly different, warmer. His muscles felt just as firm and they held her tightly, lifting her off the ground and twirling her around.

"Say you missed us, pretty girl, or I'll twirl you until you do."

"I missed you! I missed you! Please put me down!"

Jillian smacked Travis on the arm. "Put her down before she gets nauseous. I swear, men just never grow up."

Travis placed her gently on the ground and brushed his lips quickly over her forehead. Her body responded by dripping more honey from her pussy. He had kissed her as if she was a child, but her body responded all grown up. Man, she needed to have sex. It had been way too long.

Mark grabbed her suitcase and started loading it into the trunk of their high-end SUV.

"Wait! I'm riding with Jillian and my brothers."

Travis grinned and threw his arm over her shoulders, sending sparks of pleasure through her body. "You're riding with us. Since JJ and the guys have the Accord, they don't have as much luggage space. We have the SUV and have lots of luggage space. Plus, Mark and I would be all alone for the drive down to the Keys. You don't want us to be lonely, do you?"

She was going to spend the next eight hours in close quarters with them. So much for the avoidance she had planned.

"Of course I don't want you to be lonely. I'd be happy to ride with you. Jillian, are you okay with me riding with Mark and Travis?"

Jillian gave her a knowing smile. "No issue here. Have fun with the boys, but make them promise to stop if you ask. Mark's been known to avoid exits and rest stops at all costs."

Mark gave Jillian a mock scowl. "Only because you want to stop every hour. You can't get anywhere if you keep stopping."

Jillian rolled her eyes. "See? Make him promise."

Becca crossed her arms and gave him a stern look. "Promise me."

He started to protest, but Travis gave Mark's shoulder a shove. "Promise her."

Mark sighed. "I promise. I will stop no matter how often and unneeded."

Travis shook his head and ushered Becca into the car. "You'll get used to him after a while. Mark is extremely goal oriented. When he's in pursuit of something, nothing stands in his way. Just wait until he starts pursuing you."

Becca's mouth hung open as she buckled herself in the car. *They're pursuing me?*

* * * *

Becca walked along the moonlit beachfront of the hotel, her sandals dangling from her fingertips. Dinner had been a happy affair with many toasts to the bride and grooms' happiness. Somehow, Becca couldn't help but feel a little melancholy despite the jovial atmosphere. Everyone was in a loving relationship but her. It felt a little lonely. Perhaps she should have asked Josh to come with her, just as a friend, of course. She would have felt less out of place with an escort.

The ride from Plenty to Key West earlier today had taken around eight hours. Eight hours of pretending she hadn't heard Travis drop his bomb regarding Mark pursuing her. She hadn't screwed up enough courage to ask him what he meant, of course.

She had simply filed his matter-of-fact statement away in a corner of her mind, all the while chatting with them about their drive from Illinois, selling their condo, and the house they had purchased down the road from Ryan and Jack in the historic district.

Coward.

She was a great big wuss who was going to spend the next two days drooling over two men who were drooling over each other.

"Looking for Hemingway, pretty girl? You shouldn't be out here by yourself."

Travis. His voice was deep, sending shivers up and down her spine. She turned, and he wasn't alone. His hand was laced with Mark's.

They're going for a romantic walk. Together.

"I can take care of myself. I'm a black belt in Tae Kwon Do."

They both stopped in front of her, their wide shoulders blocking out the moon. Mark gave her a lopsided grin.

"Really? I love a woman who can kick some major butt. Go easy on us, okay?"

Becca pushed down her irritation. It wasn't their fault she felt like this about them. They were just being nice and probably felt a little sorry for her since she didn't have a partner.

Yet, she couldn't help feel frustrated. She was a woman who hadn't had sex in over a year. She had a major crush on two men she had just spent eight hours with confined in a car. She had breathed in their heady scent and gazed at their handsome faces. They had made her laugh and made her think. She didn't want to be their little sister or their pal. She wanted to be their woman.

"I'm trained to only use force when absolutely necessary. Are you going to make it necessary?"

"No, ma'am. Trav and I are going to behave."

Damn. That's a real shame.

Chapter 3

Travis gently entwined his fingers with hers and tugged her closer, a zing of awareness running up his arm. It was hard to be his usual cautious self when Becca was around.

"Let Mark speak for himself. I'm not sure I can behave, personally."

Her face turned up to his, and he could feel his heart clench. Her creamy skin was bathed in moonlight, lending it a luminous glow. He let his gaze wander over her mouthwatering curves, her long golden-blonde hair that hung to the middle of her back, and then it rested on her face that at the moment looked back at him with an uncertain expression. Travis could feel his frustration rise in his chest. He couldn't throw her over his shoulder and carry her to his hotel room. She was far too young and innocent for such shenanigans.

He gave Mark a quick glance and saw his own frustration reflected there. They wanted to do this right. They had planned endlessly about deepening their relationship with Becca slowly. They wanted to date her, get to know her, woo her. She deserved to be courted.

Travis gave her an encouraging smile. "Becca, we followed you out here to talk to you. When we saw your picture on Halloween, you intrigued us. Then when we met you and spent time with you at Thanksgiving and Christmas, well, we really enjoyed it. Did you enjoy spending time with us?"

"Of course I did. We've had fun. I'm glad you've moved to Plenty."

Mark smiled. "We are, too. Trav and I have wanted to simplify our lives for a long time. We've been working too hard and not enjoying life. We want to slow down and really live every day."

Mark was having trouble expressing their feelings. Travis tried to help him.

"What we're trying to say is that we're going for a brand-new start in life. We love each other. We have since our first date. But we've always felt there was one thing that would make our life more complete."

Becca looked from Travis to Mark. "What's that?"

Travis couldn't back out now. They were going to tell her what they wanted and hope she wanted the same thing, too.

"A woman to share our lives with, Becca."

Becca looked surprised. "You moved to Plenty to find a woman? I guess I...oh, shit. What I'm trying to say, and badly, is that I didn't know you, um, liked women."

Mark grabbed her other hand. "We dated both women and men before we fell for each other. So, yes, we like women, too. We especially like you."

Becca's eyes widened in surprise. "Me? You want me?"

Travis grinned at her shock. Apparently, they hadn't been too obvious. "Yes, you, sweet girl. We want to date you, court you. How do you feel about that?"

Mark ran his hand up her arm. He had a worried expression. "How do you feel about being with two guys who are also with each other? I know your dad is with Steve and Ellie, but it doesn't mean you want that kind of relationship for yourself. Will you think about it? We're crazy about you."

Becca seemed a little dazed by their declaration. Travis squeezed her hand in reassurance. "Take all the time you need to think about it. Being with two men is a big decision. Being with two men who are already in a relationship is an even bigger one. We won't rush you."

They walked in silence for a few minutes, the only sound the gentle lapping of the water on the golden sand.

They finally paused next to the hotel pool. Becca had been very quiet. Travis could feel the dread building in the pit of his stomach. She was trying to find a gentle way to let them down.

"It's okay if you don't want us that way. Mark and I are big boys. We can take the truth."

Becca turned away for a minute and then turned back. "Honestly, I'm in shock. It never occurred to me that you would want me. I'm attracted to you, too. But you're right. It just hit me that it's a big decision to get involved with two men who have been together as long as you two have. I never thought I would say this, but I do think I should think about it."

Travis brushed a stray hair from her cheek and tucked it behind her ear. "We'll wait as long as it takes. We're not interested in anyone else. Just you. You take our breath away. You look so beautiful tonight. Do you always look this beautiful?"

Becca smiled, her annoyance disappearing, and rolled her eyes. "Yes, I do. It's a curse."

Travis smiled. He couldn't help himself. He had told the truth when he said he couldn't behave. He had imagined this for months. Maybe a kiss or two would sway her in their favor, and Mark had been pushing him to take a chance. He lowered his head, his lips a hairsbreadth from hers. "Didn't the prince lift the curse with a kiss?"

* * * *

Becca caught her breath as Travis lowered his lips to hers, softly brushing against them. Her lips parted instinctively, and he swooped down, taking her lips in a soul-searing kiss that curled her toes in its intensity. His tongue played with her lips before boldly staking his claim to her mouth. Each rub of his tongue against hers sent arrows of pleasure to her clit and tightened her nipples in response.

Her hands traveled up his arms and clung to his broad shoulders. She could feel his heartbeat through his thin shirt synchronizing with her own. He lifted his head, brushing her lips once more before moving aside. She blinked in confusion before realizing Mark intended to kiss her, too.

"You look so gorgeous tonight, sweet girl. We just have to steal a kiss in the moonlight."

Mark's deep voice vibrated through his chest. She could feel it against her palm as she slid her hands up his muscular chest and around his neck to tangle in the blond hair curling at the nape of his neck. She had dreamed about kissing these men for so long, and the moment was finally here.

Mark's lips were firm as he pressed them to hers, his goatee tickling the sensitive skin around her mouth. She could smell the citrus of his cologne, and it mixed with the smell of the salty air, sending her arousal higher. His tongue traced the seam of her lips before pressing into her mouth. It explored every inch of her, tickling the roof of her mouth, before finding a sensual rhythm that made her heart beat faster and her empty pussy clench with need. Her tight nipples rubbed against the lace of her bra and honey dripped from her pussy, dampening her panties.

He finally lifted his head and gave her another smile. "Let us walk you to your room, Becca. Please."

Becca nodded, dazed at the turn of events. They walked her silently to her hotel room door before regretfully kissing her knuckles.

Travis whispered in her ear, "Dream of us, pretty girl. We're going to dream of you."

They bid her good night and left her to sleep alone in the king-size bed, restless and aroused.

Becca fell back on the bed, staring at the whirring ceiling fan. The evening had completely gotten away from her. She had vowed to stay away from them, and now she had kissed them. Not just little kisses but amazing, knock-her-out-of-her-shoes kisses, if she had been wearing shoes.

She rolled off the bed and padded over to the balcony. She stared at the ocean for long moments, taking in the streaks of moonbeams on the water. She was confused by what had happened, there was no doubt. The men wanted to have a relationship with her. It was her dream come true. Sort of.

She had been so busy fantasizing, she hadn't thought about the reality. She would be inserting herself into a relationship of fifteen years. They already had their inside jokes, their cute stories, their quirks and old arguments. Where would she fit in? She wasn't a fun toy to amuse them until they tired of her.

She knew they were good men who wouldn't deliberately play with her emotions. They seemed very sincere in their desire to have her in their life. They were in Plenty to start over, after all. Maybe she could help them create new inside jokes and cute stories. Lord knew she had her quirks. It would be fun finding out theirs.

They wanted her, and she damn well wanted them. She'd be a fool to pass up this chance to be with them, and Becca Parks was no fool. She tucked herself into bed with thoughts of the two men who slept just a few doors down the hall.

* * * *

Mark leaned back against the headboard of the hotel-room bed with a goofy grin on his face. He couldn't help himself. He'd kissed the woman of his dreams, and it had been even better than all his fantasies. And he fantasized a whole hell of a lot. He and Travis had spent the last few months making up sexy, dirty scenarios that always had the same ending—damp, sticky, and happy.

"You'd think it was your first kiss, the way you're acting."

Travis exited the bathroom wearing just a towel and a smirk.

Mark levered himself up and drank in the sight of the man he had loved for the past fifteen years. Travis was a fucking love god. Where Mark had lean muscle like a surfer, Travis had a beefier build. Not body-builder beef but enough to make Mark lick his chops in anticipation every time he saw him naked. Or in this case, almost naked.

"It was my first kiss. My first kiss with Becca. Hopefully, the first of many to come. Don't tell me your dick didn't get hard from her warm tongue in your mouth and her soft curves pressed against your body. Mine did. It's still fucking hard." Mark pointed to the bulge in his boxer shorts.

Travis whipped off his towel. "Mine went down in the cold shower, but now that you made me think about it again, it's getting hard, too. Shit, Mark."

Mark just laughed and reached out to caress Travis's hardening cock.

"It's not like I'm going to make you go to sleep unsatisfied. When have I ever done that?"

Travis rolled his eyes. "Two weeks ago, when you got called in to the hospital after that multivehicle accident on the Dan Ryan. You left me with blue balls, babe. I had to take matters into my own hands."

"Okay, but I really meant when have I left you unsatisfied when I wasn't going anywhere. You've got me all to yourself tonight. What do you plan to do with me?"

Lust flared in Travis's eyes. "On your knees, babe."

Travis's voice was hoarse but commanding. Mark slid to the floor, settling on his knees. "Lick and suck my balls. But not my cock. You need to earn it."

Mark was happy to earn the favor. His tongue lapped at Travis's crinkly sac. He opened his mouth wide and sucked while his tongue danced in circles. Travis's fingers wound through Mark's hair and tightened, letting Mark know his arousal. Travis's balls were growing tighter, and sucking them was becoming easier. Travis gave Mark's hair a pull, and his mouth popped off the now-hard sac.

"God, you're so good. Suck my cock. You know just how I like it."

Mark chuckled to himself as he sucked down Travis's length in one gulp. Mark relaxed his throat, and Travis nudged his cock further.

Mark swallowed on Travis, drawing a groan from the man of his dreams. While their crappy childhood had sent his sister into a commitment-phobia state until very recently, it had the opposite effect on Mark. He had always craved a stable home life and love. He had found it with Travis. With some luck, soon they would both have it with Becca.

Mark worked Travis's cock out of his mouth until only the reddish-purple head was still inside. He tongued the underside, pulling another groan from Travis.

Mark sucked back down and up, getting a rhythm. Travis was moving his hips in time to the stroking of Mark's tongue. If he had looked up, he knew he would see Travis with his eyes closed, head thrown back, lost in ecstasy. Mark's only goal was Travis's pleasure. Travis's hold on Mark's hair tightened painfully.

"I'm coming. Fuck, babe."

His jaws were stretched wide and his mouth was filled with his lover's delicious cock. The hot spurts of cum filled his mouth and throat. He swallowed reflexively, loving the salty taste of this man. He would never get tired of sucking Travis and feeling him come in his mouth. The feeling of power was unbelievable. He could make this wonderful man feel something this intense. Mark swallowed every drop and licked Travis's cock clean.

Travis fell back on the bed with a half groan, half laugh.

"Holy shit, babe. It just gets better and better, doesn't it?"

Mark lay next to Travis, breathing in his heady scent.

"Yeah, it does. I love you."

Travis nuzzled Mark's neck. "I love you, too. And I think it's your turn."

Travis kissed his way down Mark's body, sending sparks of pleasure to his cock and balls. Travis quickly stripped Mark of his boxer shorts and fondled his balls. He was already close to blowing his load.

"Do you think Becca likes to suck cock, babe?"

Travis's tongue licked him from balls to tip. Mark moaned at the sensation and the erotic visual of Becca on her knees sucking his cock with her hot mouth.

Mark shook his head. "Doesn't matter. I've got you for that."

Travis's laughter sent vibrations up his dick.

"I guess you do. I guess I got you for that, too."

Travis teased Mark with his tongue until he was begging to be finished.

"Suck me, man. I need to come."

His balls were hard as rocks and his cock was painful.

"I love it when you beg."

Travis engulfed the head of Mark's cock with his mouth, licking and sucking until Mark couldn't hold back his release. He grabbed Travis by the hair and shoved his dick into his welcoming warmth, shooting his cum deep in Travis's mouth. Mark watched Travis's throat work as he swallowed every drop. They both collapsed on the bed, satiated for now.

It was Travis who broke the silence.

"I really hope she likes to suck cock."

Mark couldn't stop the laughter at Travis's hopeful tone. Despite Travis's natural reticence, he couldn't quell the hope that Becca was the one they had been waiting for. Mark rolled away to pull the covers over them.

"Why don't we ask her tomorrow? 'Hey, Becca, we'd like to take you out on a date, and oh, by the way, are you for or against blow jobs?'"

Travis scowled at him. "This is exactly why she may not fall in love with us. We're way too raunchy and dirty for her. She's ten years younger than us and, hell, living in a small town, she may be pretty innocent. I'm not saying she's a virgin, but she may not appreciate our dirty minds or mouths."

Mark winced. Despite their highly educated state, they were really just a couple of guys who liked to drink beer and watch hockey. They needed to clean things up for Becca.

"You're right. We need to stop thinking about blow jobs and think about how to show her what great guys we are. How we can take care of her and make her happy. We need to get a plan."

Travis yawned. "Tomorrow. Tomorrow, we'll get a plan. Tonight we sleep."

Mark yawned, too. "Yeah, tomorrow's soon enough. Becca's going to be ours. She's going to fall head over heels for us."

Mark looked over, and Travis was already snoring. Loudly. Making Becca love them might be harder than they originally thought.

Chapter 4

Becca sipped her mimosa slowly. She loved the taste, but it always gave her a headache if she didn't drink it daintily. She hid her snort at the thought. Dainty she wasn't.

She let her gaze wander across the deck of the hotel pool. The reception was in full swing. The sunrise ceremony had been incredibly beautiful. She had sniffled into her handkerchief as her father, Steve, and Ellie vowed to love, honor, and cherish each other. Then each of them had spoken about what made them love the other two and how their relationship wouldn't be complete without all of them in it.

Travis, especially, seemed to have an intense expression on his face during the ceremony. Becca wondered if he would be as intense when making love.

Jillian and Cassie threw themselves down in chairs next to Becca. They were breathless from dancing with their men. Becca felt a pang of jealousy but pushed it away. She wasn't that type of person. She was truly happy for them. They had both been through so much they deserved all the happiness in the world.

Cassie had been stalked for years by a man who wanted to possess her. He had followed her to Plenty and died, drowning in the limestone quarries. Jillian's parents had fought like cats and dogs, leaving her afraid of love and commitment. Both women had certainly found both when they moved to Plenty last fall. Cassie would be marrying Zach and Chase during spring break, and Jillian was trying to set a date to marry Ryan and Jack.

Becca sighed. Maybe she just wasn't the type to inspire a grand passion in a man. Jillian plucked two mimosas from the tray of a passing waiter, handing one of them to Cassie.

"What was that heavy sigh for? And don't try and tell us nothing. You've been acting weird all damn day. Spill it, or we tell that waiter over there you want to go skinny-dipping with him."

Becca looked at where Jillian was pointing and then shrugged. "I don't think I'm his type, so go ahead. He looks more interested in your husbands-to-be. Better watch out."

Jillian took a gulp of her drink and chuckled. "My men are way too worn out to even look anywhere else but at me. Just last night, we—"

Becca held up her hand. "Stop. For the love of all that's holy, stop. They're my brothers. Ick."

Jillian popped a chocolate-covered strawberry from Becca's plate in her mouth.

"Okay, okay. But I don't think it's the fact they're your brothers that's bothering you. I think it's the fact you're not getting any."

Becca loved Jillian's no-holds-barred attitude about life.

"*Any*? Pray tell, what do you mean *any*?"

Cassie rolled her eyes at both of them.

"I'm sure Becca is fine, Jillian. Sex isn't everything."

"It's not nothing, either. Becca needs a man."

"Stop, both of you. The fact is Jillian's right."

Jillian gave Cassie a smug look, which only served to make Cassie stick out her tongue at Jillian. They argued like sisters but loved each other dearly. Becca felt fortunate to have been drawn into their warm circle of friendship.

Cassie looked around the reception. "Well, there don't seem to be too many candidates here."

Becca looked around in puzzlement. "Candidates for what?"

Cassie was still looking. "You know, a freaky-deaky one-night stand."

Jillian planted her face in her palm with a groan.

"Becca does not need a one-night stand, for heaven's sake. Although it's not the worst idea in the world should other options be closed to her. What she really needs is a little M and T."

Becca almost choked on her drink. "Did you say S & M?"

Jillian laughed. "No, I said M and T, although if you're into it, go for it. I don't judge. I was talking about Mark and Travis. You need them. They need you. It's really perfect, you know."

Becca felt her face get warm. She had tried to hide her attraction to them, but apparently it had been an epic fail.

"They don't need me. They have each other."

That was the heart of the matter. They would never need her.

"Of course they need you. They're definitely in lust. I saw the looks on their faces last night. Their eyes followed you everywhere. So what are you waiting for? They've been staring at you again since the ceremony."

So she hadn't imagined it.

Becca set down her champagne flute. These were her best friends.

"Actually, they told me last night they want to have a relationship with me. I'm not sure how I feel about it."

Cassie looked at her in amazement. "You don't know how you feel about it? What are you confused about exactly? You're attracted, they're attracted. You're all free to do as you please. What's the issue? Is it Josh?"

Becca started shredding the paper napkin on the table.

"No, it's not Josh. He's a great guy, but not for me. Well, they're not really free, are they? They're together. They have been for years. What if I'm just something to spice up their relationship after fifteen years together? What if I'm just a chew toy or something for them?"

It was Jillian's turn to look amazed. "A *chew toy*? What the hell? Mark and Travis would never use you like that, Becca. They're good men."

"I know they are. I'm not saying they would do this on purpose. But how long have they been looking for a woman? And how long will they want me?"

Jillian tried to answer, but Becca cut her off. "You both are lucky. Your men aren't in love with each other. You're the center of their world. You're their whole life." Becca's voice dropped to a whisper. "My whole life I've lived in the shadow of my sheriff and firefighter older brothers. Just once I want to be the center of someone's life. Don't you see? They're already the center of each other's lives. Where would I fit in?"

Cassie grabbed her hand and squeezed. "There's room for you in the center. Look at every ménage relationship in this town. The woman is always the focal point. Look at your Dad and Steve with Ellie. They'd both die for her. Didn't you listen to the vows today? In a ménage, all the parties play an equal but important role. Your role wouldn't be minor to Mark's and Travis's."

Becca let out a long breath. "I want to believe that. I did listen to the vows today. God, I feel so selfish. I really want to give this a try."

Jillian put her arm around Becca's shoulders and hugged her. "You are not fucking selfish. Every woman wants to be the center of her man's world. Listen, I learned this the hard way with your brothers. Talk to them. Tell them what you're thinking. If I had had the courage to just talk to Ryan and Jack, we would have been together a lot sooner."

Becca threw down the shredded napkin. "They'll think I'm insane."

Cassie shook her head. "No, they'll think you took the issue seriously. They need to inspect their motivations closely, too."

Becca slumped in the chair. "Okay, I'll talk to them. Tomorrow." Becca raised her champagne glass. "Today we celebrate, tomorrow I'll humiliate myself."

Jillian clinked her glass with Becca's.

"Look on the bright side. If you drink enough now, you don't have to wait until tomorrow to humiliate yourself."

* * * *

She hadn't drank nearly enough. Just the one mimosa. Now the men were heading straight for her with matching determined expressions on their faces. There was nowhere to hide. She wouldn't have the luxury of waiting until the morning.

Travis grabbed her hand and kissed the knuckles. "Dance with me, sweetheart?"

Becca looked hesitantly at Mark, but he waved her on with a smile.

"I'll stick to the sidelines. I have an old football injury."

Mark rubbed his knee. Travis pulled her toward the dance area.

"Yeah, a football injury that only flares up when there's dancing. I'll take good care of Becca, while you sit there all alone."

Travis pulled her close to his warm body. His scent surrounded her, and she couldn't stop her body's natural reaction. Her nipples were hard beneath the thin silk dress she wore. He was holding her so tightly he could probably feel them through his dress shirt.

"Does he really have a football injury? It would be a little ironic, since he's an orthopedic surgeon."

"Naw, he has no rhythm. It's embarrassing. He can't even snap his fingers to a beat. It's pathetic. And he's not an orthopedic surgeon any longer. He's a general practitioner now. We've left the rat race behind us."

"Plenty can still be busy. This is the first real vacation I've had in a year. A few days here and there don't really count."

Travis's warm hand caressed the skin exposed by the low back of her dress. She felt the tingles all the way to her pussy. His thighs brushed hers as they sensuously moved together. He was a great dancer.

"Mark and I will have to make sure this is a memorable one."

"It already is. It's not very often two men ask me to date them."

"That I find hard to believe. What are those men in Plenty thinking?"

"They're thinking I'm like a little sister to them."

Travis leaned forward and brushed her ear with his lips, sending a shiver down her spine. "I don't feel the least brotherly toward you at all. Not one bit."

Becca pulled back and looked into Travis's soft brown eyes. "I think we probably all three need to talk. I have a few concerns or questions, you could say."

Travis nodded and then held her hand as they walked back to Mark.

"Let's get your questions answered, then. Let's grab Mark and find somewhere quiet to talk."

* * * *

Travis held his breath as the three of them headed for Becca's hotel room. It was the only place they could find where it was quiet and they could talk in private. The brunch and reception downstairs was in full swing and looked like it could go for hours.

Becca unlocked the door and headed in first, switching on every light in the room despite the bright sunlight pouring through the sliding glass windows. Apparently, she was a little nervous about them being there. They needed to assure her nothing would happen today. They were going to court her like gentlemen. She deserved no less. Besides, Travis was looking forward to romancing her. He and Mark never really got classically romantic with each other. Travis wanted to buy Becca roses, dance in the moonlight, and take her to classy restaurants. If only they had one in Plenty.

Becca stood stiffly in front of the balcony doors.

"So, I guess I have some questions. If you don't mind answering them."

Mark sat on the end of the bed while Travis grabbed one of the two chairs at the table. He grabbed Becca's hand and tugged her down into the other chair.

"Relax, sweetheart. We're going to be perfect gentlemen today. Nothing is going to happen unless you agree to it. So, ask away."

Becca looked slightly more relaxed. "How long have you known you wanted a ménage? Why do you want a ménage? I mean, you guys have been together for years."

Mark and Travis exchanged a look. Travis got Mark's message immediately. The answers were obviously important to Becca, so Travis, the attorney, would make their case.

* * * *

Mark sat back to watch Travis work his magic. If he could sway a grouchy, sequestered jury, he could convince Becca they weren't just a couple of bored guys looking to score a piece of ass.

Travis held Becca's hands and looked straight into her eyes.

"Mark and I love each other very much. We have from practically the first moment we met. Do you know how we met?"

Becca shook her head.

"Our girlfriends were roommates."

Her brow knitted. "Your girlfriends were roommates? Those poor girls! They thought you liked them when all the time you only wanted each other?"

Travis shook his head.

"No, we did like them. We were dating very nice girls at the time. They wanted to go on a double date, and that's how we met. I knew Mark was the one before the end of the evening. We transitioned out of our relationships and started dating each other."

Becca crossed her arms over her chest and pursed her lips.

"Transitioned? Is that a legal term for dumping someone?"

For the first time in fifteen years, Travis seemed at a loss for words. It appeared convincing one cute little blonde was a whole lot different than convincing twelve jurors. Mark decided to step in.

"We didn't dump them, sweetheart. In fact, I dated Lori for about a month afterward. She could tell I wasn't that into her and dumped me. As for Travis's girlfriend, Stacey, it was very casual between them. They dated a few more times and drifted apart. I can assure you no one was heartbroken. I'm still good friends with Lori and her husband."

Becca's body language seemed to relax.

"That sounds better. So when you were both out of the relationships, you started dating?"

Travis nodded. "We were together from that very first date. Mark and I went to a Blackhawks game. We've been a couple since then. Our lives are great. But as we were building our careers and decorating our home, something was always missing."

Mark leaned forward and grabbed her hand. "You. You were missing."

Becca raised her eyebrows. "Me? You were looking for me? How many girls did you audition before you found me?"

Mark could hear the doubt in her voice. "We have been with women through the years, every now and then. We missed having a woman in our lives. But they never fit in with us. The three personalities, well, they didn't mesh. You, on the other hand, meshed from the moment we met you. You center and balance our relationship, Becca. We need you to feel complete."

Travis brought her fingers to his lips. "We didn't even know living in a ménage was an option until Cassie and Jillian moved to Plenty. We thought our lives would always have something missing. You can't imagine how we felt when we met you. We just want a chance to show you we're not playing around with your emotions. We're serious about making this ménage work."

Becca was worrying her bottom lip. "Are you bored?"

The question took Mark aback. "Bored? Are you asking if we're looking for a third because we're bored with our relationship? Oh, fuck no."

Travis seconded. "Hell no, pretty girl. Mark and I have a very good relationship, and yes, the sex is still hot. Of course, with you we think it will be scorching."

Becca's face turned a lovely shade of pink.

"You say I balance you. How do I do that?"

Travis pointed to Mark. "Mark, here? Outside of the operating room he's a grab-life-by-the-balls kind of guy. It can make me crazy sometimes. You'd think after all these years I would be used to it, but, shit, I'm not. Do you know he once signed us up to climb Mount Everest? I'm not fucking climbing a mountain where most people die trying it."

Mark pointed to Travis. "Do you know this guy is so cautious and unspontaneous we have to plan a dinner out at least three hours in advance? And he hates to try anything new. He has to think about it for a month or two before he will try anything. This move to Plenty is the first semispontaneous thing we've done in fifteen years. Even then, we'd been talking about making a change in our lives for the last five years. He can drive me up a wall."

Becca laughed. "And how am I supposed to help this situation? You both sound crazy."

Travis grinned. "We're extremes of the spectrum. You're nicely in the middle. Of course, we realize you might have some extremes, too. We hope we'll all balance out in the end."

Becca's expression grew serious. "What if we don't?"

Mark pulled her onto his lap. "That's what dating is for—to find out these things. We just want a chance to get to know you better and for you to get to know us. As we said last night, we know getting involved in an established relationship won't be easy. But look on the bright side, Trav and I have already worked out our issues over the years."

Becca looked from Mark to Travis and back. "Okay, we'll date. I can't deny I feel something for both of you. If you're willing to take a chance on me, I'm willing to take a chance on both of you."

Mark felt the happiness swell in his chest. "You won't regret this, sweetheart. Trav and I are going to take very good care of you."

Becca ran her hand down his arm. "How about starting now? We should kiss on the agreement."

* * * *

A light flared in Mark's eyes, and she felt a curl of arousal through her belly. She shouldn't tempt fate with kissing these men in her hotel room, but she couldn't stop herself. She had been thinking about those kisses from last night all day.

Mark pulled her closer, his intoxicating scent surrounding her. He smelled like sun, ocean, and man. It sent her hormones skittering and her heart pounding. She ran her hands up his arms, over his wide shoulders, and around his neck. His lips were oh so close to her own when she felt a second set of lips caressing the bare skin of her shoulder. Travis pushed her long hair to her other shoulder and rained openmouthed kisses on the nape of her neck. A moan escaped from her lips just as Mark captured them with his own.

His kiss was everything. His lips fit perfectly with her own. His tongue explored her mouth sensually, rubbing against hers and playing tag. When he finally lifted his head, her breath was coming in pants and her heart was beating out of control. Her nipples were painfully tight and her pussy was dripping honey. Travis nipped and licked his way from her neck down the exposed flesh of her shoulders, then back up to her waiting lips.

Travis's kiss dominated her senses. She could feel his hard muscles underneath her palms. His warm scent tickled her nose. His mouth and tongue staked his claim as her man. She had never felt so small and feminine as with these men. The curl of arousal that had started with Mark coiled tighter, and she pressed herself against Travis, her pussy clenching in desperation. She needed these men inside of her. Her fingers dug into Travis's shoulders.

Travis pulled back, breathing heavy, his expression stamped with desire.

"We feel the same, little one. But we made a promise to you to act like gentlemen. If you're ready to make love right now, we're ready. But I'm not sure you're ready to jump into bed with us quite yet."

Was she ready? She had known them for a while now. She wanted them, and it had been so long since she had made love with a man. She pressed herself against Travis again in invitation.

"I want you, both of you."

Both men looked surprised, but passion quickly took its place. They wanted her, too. Travis tugged her down on the bed with him, his hands burning everywhere he touched. Mark joined them, pressing his hard cock into the seam of her ass while nibbling on her shoulders. She gasped at the twin sensations. She lost herself in just feeling the pleasure with these men. The brush of Mark's fingers, the tickle of Travis's hair sent her spiraling higher. But she wasn't so far gone she didn't hear the knock on her hotel-room door.

"Hey, girl! Are you in there?"

Jillian.

"Becca, are you in there?"

Cassie.

Becca pulled away regretfully. She had forgotten she had promised Jillian and Cassie she would sightsee with them after the brunch.

"Yeah, hold on."

Mark and Travis straightened her clothes. Somehow Mark had managed to get the zip of her dress halfway down without her noticing. She opened the door and stood in the opening, not wanting to reveal the two men inside.

"Hey, listen, I'll be down in a minute. I haven't changed yet."

She wasn't fooling anyone. Jillian took one look at her guilty expression and gave her a knowing smile.

"We'll wait in the lobby. Give Mark and Trav a kiss from me."

Becca closed the door and leaned her forehead on the smooth wood. The girls had very few secrets from one another, and the men weren't going to be one of them apparently. She turned back to see them practically holding their sides to keep in their laughter.

"Find this amusing, do you?"

Mark grinned. "A little. My sister has a dirty mind, babe. No way was she not going to take one look at your face and know we were up to no good in here. I hope you're not ashamed of us."

Becca sighed. "Of course not, it just would have been nice to have some privacy. Although, living in a small town should have taught me a long time ago that privacy is hard to come by."

Travis chuckled. "I promise, babe, when the time comes for us to make love, we'll have lots of privacy. Deal?"

"Deal."

The men headed for the door.

"No kiss good-bye?"

Mark pushed an errant strand of hair from her face. "If we kiss you, we won't get out of here. Have fun with Jillian and Cassie. Motorcade to Plenty leaves at nine tomorrow morning. Don't be late, sweetheart."

Mark gave her a wink as they headed for their own room. Becca locked up behind them and leaned against the door in a daze. If the men were half as good at making love as they were at kissing, she was in a hell of a lot of trouble.

Chapter 5

"I want to hear all about the wedding. Was it very romantic?"

Becca was back in Plenty, delivering lunch to Addie and recounting the weekend for her entertainment. Becca sat down with a sigh and stretched her legs out.

"It was romantic. The ceremony took place on Bridle Lane at sunrise. They all three seemed so in love. They said traditional vows but also wrote some of their own."

The three were now off on a ten-day honeymoon to Hawaii, and Becca had to admit her own envy. She would love to be off to a tropical paradise with two men she loved.

"They're in Hawaii for their honeymoon. The way Dad and Steve looked at Ellie—it was wonderful."

"Were there lots of flowers? I love flowers."

Addie was more interested in hearing the bridal details than eating the pot roast and asparagus Becca had delivered.

Becca nodded. "Oh yeah, lots of flowers, especially at the reception. Big tropical arrangements with amazing colors. They had tiger lilies. I love tiger lilies."

Addie nodded in agreement. "Tiger lilies are lovely. What did you wear?"

"Black dress with red flowers. It had spaghetti straps and a low back. I looked hot."

Becca giggled as she remembered the way Mark and Travis had looked at her. She really wasn't hot and sexy, but they certainly made her feel that way.

Addie beamed. "I'm sure you did. You're a lovely young woman. Any luck with the fellas when you were there?"

Becca was a terrible liar. She knew her expression was a dead giveaway.

"You must have had some luck. You have a wonderfully guilty expression on your face. Did you get lucky?"

"Addie!"

Becca's face flamed at Addie's outrageous query. Addie just chuckled and waved off her embarrassment.

"Oh heavens, you young people can be so prudish at times. At my age, we don't have time to beat around the bush and talk in code. Sex is a wonderful thing. It's even better when you can share it with someone you have feelings for."

Addie's eyes twinkled as she leaned forward. "But it's still pretty good if you don't."

Becca planted her forehead on the cool surface of the kitchen table and groaned. Finally, Becca looked up with a grin. "TMI, Addie."

Addie leaned back in her chair with a laugh. "I know that means Too Much Information. I thought you liked my stories."

"I do. Especially when we stick to people I don't know and will never meet."

"Right now, we're talking about you, Becca Parks. What happened?"

Addie wasn't going to give up. Besides, she trusted Addie and valued her advice. Becca told her about Mark, Travis, and their request to start dating her and sharing their lives.

Addie looked thoughtful as Becca finished her story.

"Sounds like those boys have some strong feelings for you, Becca. Of course, you are the sweetest girl I know. They seem like good men. What's next?"

"I'm not sure. They said they wanted to court me. I don't think I've ever been courted before. At least not formally. Heck, most guys in Plenty were afraid to ask me out. Between my dad, Ryan, and Jack, they'd get the third degree so bad I'd be lucky to ever see them again. Let's face it, everyone in town knows Ryan and Jack's reputation. And, of course, mine as their innocent little sister. That's a reputation I love—the afterthought."

Addie patted her hand. "I know you've lived in the shadow of your brothers for a long time. They're good, hardworking men. It's easy for people to pay attention to the sheriff or a firefighter. You do good work for Plenty, too, Becca. You never call attention to the charity work you do for the city. And I happen to know you do loads for this town. Relationships are different. If you're truly open and honest with them, they'll see all the ways you shine. You won't need to fight for their attention or love."

"Truly open and honest, huh?"

Addie smiled. "It's the secret to a lasting ménage. All the good relationships in Plenty had that one thing in common." Addie picked up her fork and picked at her asparagus with a grimace. "And hot monkey sex, too, of course."

Becca groaned. "TMI, Addie. TMI."

* * * *

"Come on in, guys, and help yourself to a beer. We'll start the game in a few minutes. Ryan's not here yet."

Jack slapped Mark on the back and waved him toward the kitchen. Zach was already there drinking a longneck and munching on hot wings. Mark and Travis were hanging out with Zach, Chase, Jack, and Ryan for a Monday-night game of poker. Becca was at her regular Monday-night dinner with the girls.

"I'm glad we decided to have our own Monday-night ritual, since the women have theirs."

Chase's eyebrows almost went up to his hairline as the heat from the wings singed his tongue. He quickly drank a big gulp of beer. Zach shook his head and laughed.

"Careful, bro, those wings are hot. We sure are glad you and Travis moved here, Mark. We didn't have enough for a game before. Are you settling into the new house?"

He and Travis had purchased a home in the historic district just down the street from Ryan, Jack, and soon to be Jillian. It needed a lot of work, but they were both looking forward to making it a real home. Hopefully, a real home with Becca.

Travis nodded. "Yes, although we'd forgotten how much work moving and renovating can be. We love the house, but it does need work. We're really glad you and Chase are going to be available to help us with some of the heavier stuff."

Zach grinned. "We wouldn't have it any other way. We're almost done with the renovations on Charlie's pizza parlor. They're planning a big grand reopening as soon as we've finished. Shouldn't be more than a week or two."

Travis popped a few chips in his mouth. "I can't wait. She had fantastic pizza the one time we were there, just before the fire. What ever happened to Jenny, the young girl who set the fire?"

Zach turned toward the front door. "That question is better directed at Ryan, who looks like he's finally arrived."

Sheriff Ryan Parks headed into the kitchen and accepted a beer with a grin. Still in his uniform, he must have just got off work.

Chase shook his head with a wry smile. "About damn time you got here. I thought we'd have to call nine-one-one and report a crime."

Ryan took a long draw from his beer. "Damn, that hits the spot. It's been a long fucking day. I think everyone in Plenty reported a crime today."

Jack chuckled. "Was it Tom again? Is the missus on the warpath?"

When Tom's wife wasn't speaking to him, he liked to commit petty crimes so he could argue with Ryan or the judge.

Ryan blew out a breath. "Tom was only one of my problems today. Although he sure as hell didn't help matters. Damn fool backed his car into the gate of the drive-in as a protest against the movies Max has been showing lately. Says he wants the Creature Features back on Saturday nights instead of the chick flicks. Max was pissed as hell about his gate, and when I got there he was cussin' a blue streak threatening to back into Tom's garage door. Fuck. Sometimes they don't pay me enough to do this job."

Jack slapped his brother on the back. "Just have another beer, bro. Your long day is over, and lady luck is on, well, my side anyway."

Mark laughed. "You know what they say, Jack. Lucky in love, and all that."

Jack's gaze traveled to the fireplace mantle and the picture of Ryan, Jack, and Jillian from the Christmas party in the park just a few months ago.

"Hell yeah, I'm lucky in love. I'm marrying the most beautiful woman in Plenty."

Zach and Chase both shook their heads. "Nope. We are, and soon, too."

Mark wouldn't be outdone. "Becca's the most beautiful woman in Plenty. Not that Jillian and Cassie aren't gorgeous. They are."

Four heads whipped toward him in unison.

Ryan gave him a speculative look. "Is there something you want to tell me about my baby sister and you, Mark? Are you seeing her? If you are, you need to state your intentions now, like a man."

Mark pulled Travis to his side. "We will state our intentions. They're honorable, Ryan. We care about Becca. We've asked her to date us with the intention to make something permanent. We wouldn't offer her anything less."

Ryan turned to Travis. "Are you in agreement with this?"

Travis nodded. "Absolutely. We have feelings for Becca. We just want the chance to get to know her and for her to get to know us. We want this to be a forever thing. We're not fucking around with her. I promise."

Ryan gave them a hard stare. It was clear why he was the sheriff.

"If either of you break my little sister's heart, I will cheerfully kick your asses from here to Chicago and back. Do I make myself clear?"

Jack stepped in. "Pardon my brother, he can be a caveman at times. What he means to say is, don't fucking play with her emotions. If she sheds one fucking tear over you two, there isn't a corner of this earth far enough to escape our wrath."

Zach rolled his eyes. "That was less caveman? Knock that shit off, right now. Becca is a grown woman. I didn't see Mark getting all up in your business when you were dating his sister. Especially you, Jack. Did you make Jillian cry with your stupid antics?"

Jack had the grace to look ashamed. "Aw shit, Zach, I didn't mean to. You know Jillian's the only woman in the world to me. Sorry, man. I guess we're so used to taking care of Becca we got carried away."

Jack pushed Ryan's shoulder. "Didn't we get carried away?"

Ryan's mouth twisted. "Fuck. We got carried away. Since Mom died, I guess we've gone into superprotective mode. We know you're good guys. Shit, I'm sorry. You never gave us any hell about dating Jillian."

Mark and Travis glanced at each other and then back at Jack and Ryan. Travis shook his head. "Don't worry about it. I think it's great Becca has two brothers who love her this much. We won't disrespect her. You have our word."

The men shook hands while Zach set up the cards and poker chips.

"Ryan, Travis asked me about Jenny. He wanted to know what happened to her after she confessed to setting those fires. I said you probably had the latest."

The men sat down, and Zach started dealing the first hand.

"Jenny pled out. She'll get intense psychiatric treatment in a state hospital for the next few years. What was surprising was to find out that she's done this before dear old Jack here. Apparently, when she was at the University of Florida she did some minor vandalism to get attention from another guy she was obsessed with. Poor bastard. She stalked him for an entire year before getting kicked out of school for bad grades. She returned to Plenty and got odd jobs before getting the waitress job at the coffee shop. "

Jack picked up his cards. "She almost got Leah and Jillian killed. Seems like she should get more than psychiatric treatment."

Ryan shrugged. "Be realistic, Jack. I doubt the facility she's going to be living in is a country club. She's paying for her crimes."

Ryan took another draw from his longneck.

"You're lucky. You won't have any of the arson drama with Becca that we did with Jillian or the stalker drama that Zach and Chase had with Cassie. Becca is a quiet, homebody, no-drama kind of girl. Your relationship should be smooth sailing."

Mark gave Travis a smile. Now they were here in Plenty, everything was going to go exactly as they had planned.

* * * *

Becca and Jillian were on the coffee table in Becca's living room dancing to "We Got the Beat" by the Go-Go's. Becca twirled around and did a shimmy shake just as Jillian hopped off the table laughing. She collapsed on the couch next to Cassie, who was laughing so hard she was holding her stomach.

"You guys are crazy! Jillian, get back up there and dance with Becca!"

Becca laughed, breathless and giddy from their Monday girls'-night fun.

"I just love these eighties tunes. I was born twenty years too late."

Becca landed in a heap on the couch and took a gulp of her fuzzy navel. The girls were having an eighties-themed evening after their Monday-night dinner tradition. Their hair was teased high and streaked with some fun punk-pink streaks. Jillian munched on a nacho and pulled a face.

"I'm not so sure about that. Can you imagine trying to have big hair every single day? The infrastructure alone must have taken forever. And I have a lot of hair!"

Becca shrugged. "I'm a hairdresser. I do hair all day long."

Cassie grinned. "And for that, we are most grateful. Enough about big hair, already. What happened with Mark and Travis at the reception?"

Becca took another gulp of her drink. "We've decided to date."

Cassie and Jillian exchanged a look. Jillian grabbed Becca's glass and set it at the far end of the coffee table. "You're not getting that drink back until we get some damn details. Spill it."

Becca rolled her eyes. "I was almost done with it anyway. So, I asked them some questions and we decided to date. You know, see if we like each other."

It was Cassie's turn to roll her eyes. "Like each other? You guys were about to hump each others' legs at the wedding. The air was positively thick with sexual tension. Did you, um, release any of that tension? Before we so rudely interrupted, that is."

"It was rude, wasn't it? And no, not really. We kissed. It was…hot. Very hot. If you hadn't interrupted, well, things would have gotten interesting. But I'm actually kind of glad you did interrupt. I was okay with sleeping with them that day, but now I'm even more sure."

Jillian pounced. "Ooooo, the first-time sex is always so hot. Your brothers about singed my panties off. So you're ready now?"

Becca felt her face get warm. "Definitely. It's not like I haven't gotten to know them these last months. We've spent a lot of time together during their visits. If you count both Thanksgiving and Christmas, I've actually gone out on several dates with them. I just wasn't alone with them very often. All of us were there—shopping, biking, playing bingo, hanging out at the diner or the coffee shop.

Let's not forget the night at your condo when we all played Monopoly and Travis kicked everyone's ass."

Jillian chuckled. "Travis always wins. You might as well get used to it. I don't know how he does it, but he does. You don't have to justify your feelings for Mark and Travis. Sometimes, you just know."

Cassie handed Becca her drink. "You don't have to justify it to me, either. You have spent quite a bit of time with them when they were here. It's no shame to want to sleep with them. If they weren't like brothers to me, and I wasn't engaged to two of the hottest men in the world, I'd be all over Mark and Travis. Go for it. We're cheering you on."

Becca groaned. "That's a picture I don't need. You and Jillian sitting next to the bed with pom-poms doing cheers. Spare me the visual."

Cassie and Jillian fell into peals of laughter. Jillian wiped the tears from her eyes. "No worries, Becca. The last place I want to be is watching my brothers have sex. We'll cheer you on virtually."

Cassie nudged Becca. "Just do something kinky and dirty, okay? You're representing the three of us. We're not the fucking girls next door."

Becca smiled. The boys were going to learn just how not the girl next door she was.

* * * *

Becca rang the doorbell at Mark and Travis's house bright and early Saturday morning. They planned to take her for dinner tonight, but she had offered to help them paint their living room and dining room today. By the time they finished painting, they would be ready for an evening out.

A smiling Travis answered the door. "Hey, sweetie, you're here early. Come on in and join us for breakfast."

"You said early, so I'm here early."

Travis waved to a barstool pulled up to the kitchen counter.

"Relax, and let me get you some coffee. I know we said early, and then I wondered what you considered early. I know you work a lot of late nights at the salon, so you might sleep in."

Becca hopped up on the barstool, avoiding a stack of flooring samples towering near her chair. Partially unpacked boxes, furniture covered in sheets, and a wall torn down to the studs gave the house a decidedly chaotic feel.

"I wish I could sleep in. I'm one of those annoying early birds."

Travis laughed. "You can keep Mark company then. He's always up with the birds."

Becca looked around.

"Where is Mark? He's not stuck under one of these boxes, is he?"

Travis pulled a face. "It's awful, isn't it? I can hardly stand to live here. We need to get moving on all these renovations before I lose my mind. And Mark ran to the hardware store to pick up the paint. He should be here any minute. In the meantime, have some bacon and toast. I can fix you some eggs if you like."

Becca shook her head. "I had some cereal this morning, but I never turn down bacon."

"A girl after my own heart. Don't let Dr. Health Nut talk you out of eating bacon once in a while. The way he acts, you would think bacon was responsible for the bubonic plague."

"Dr. Steve is the same way. He makes sure the meals I deliver are always healthy and balanced. Some of the patients get so frustrated. Sometimes you just need a cookie, you know?"

"I agree. I know you deliver meals to those who have health issues. That must be very rewarding, sweetheart. It just goes to show what a big heart you have."

"I love doing it. There's one woman I deliver to who's my favorite. I know I shouldn't have a favorite, but I do. Her name is Addie. She tells great stories about the history of Plenty. I don't know if any of them are true of course, but they're great stories."

Travis refilled her coffee with a smile. "She sounds like a great old lady. I'd love to meet her sometime."

Becca smiled back. Addie would love to have a couple of handsome men visit her. "She'd love that, too. She doesn't get much company. Her nephew visits now and again, but he's…"

"He's what?"

Becca exhaled slowly. She didn't like speaking ill of someone, especially someone she barely knew.

"He's…creepy. Kind of. Well, he gave me the creeps the one time I met him. I think he was kind of coming on to me. And hello, so not my type. He was talking to her about a guaranteed investment. I don't think they really have those, do they?"

Travis frowned. "Well, there are bonds and things that return a fixed rate. I'm sure that's what he meant. You wouldn't want an elderly woman to take any sort of risks with her money."

Becca nodded slowly. She wasn't feeling the trust when it came to Randall.

"And he better not be your type. Hopefully, Mark and I are the only two men who fit your type."

Travis hooked his arm around Becca's waist and pulled her closer. She could smell the clean spice from his morning shower. She let her hands slide up his chest and around his neck. She gave him her best pout.

"What's a girl to do when only two men in the world are her type? And they live in Chicago, too."

Travis leaned forward so his lips were a hairsbreadth from hers.

"Be so wonderful and amazing they move to a small town in Florida, that's what."

Becca laughed. "I'm not the real reason you moved to Plenty, but I'll pretend that I am."

Travis gave her a teasing smile. "Well, that's true, but you've certainly turned out to be the best reason."

His hand drifted up her back to tangle in her long blonde hair and his lips fused with hers, sending her blood pressure soaring and her nipples spiking against the lace of her bra. He lifted his head and gave her a cocky smile.

"You're the only woman who fits our type, too, sweetheart. We've been waiting for you."

Chapter 6

Mark threw down the paintbrush with a tired sigh. The walls were finally done. The soft green color was perfect with the dark wood and red accents. Becca really had an eye for color. It was a good thing, too. Mark had returned from the hardware store with four gallons of paint that had obviously disturbed Becca.

She had tried to be so sweet about not liking the color. She had chewed her bottom lip, her brows knitted together in concern, before softly voicing her concerns about the brightness of the yellow he had purchased. One swipe of the paint on the bare wall had told the story. It looked practically neon. Becca had accompanied Mark back to the hardware store, where she had chosen a soft heather green.

They had only stopped briefly to eat some leftover fried chicken from the diner for lunch. Now Mark wanted to sweep their woman off her feet and feed her dinner and then maybe a movie at the drive-in. Max was playing a Thin Man movie double feature this weekend. Becca had never seen any Thin Man movies, and Travis wanted to introduce her to William Powell and Myrna Loy's famous movie series.

Becca was lounging on the sheet-covered couch giggling at something Travis was saying. Mark let his gaze roam from the tips of her pink-painted toenails to the top of her golden hair. She was gorgeous. Her curves were mouthwateringly generous. She wasn't one of those women who lived on celery sticks and water. Those curves were currently filling out a pair of old cutoff shorts and a black T-shirt. His mind wandered to an image of Becca on her back while he fucked her breasts, coming all over her chest and neck. It was an erotic image that immediately sent blood rushing to his cock. It pressed against the button fly of his faded jeans, reminding him how long it had been since he'd had a woman.

He and Travis liked to be with women now and then. Even before meeting Becca, they had become discouraged about ever finding a woman to share and hadn't slept with one in over a year. After meeting her at Thanksgiving, the idea of any other woman was an anathema to them. They only wanted her.

"This color is great. Thank goodness you came over today, or we would have had the ugliest living room and dining room in Plenty."

Travis gave Becca a teasing smile, which she returned.

"Don't sell yourself short. I think they would have been the ugliest rooms in the entire state of Florida, not just Plenty."

Mark loved how she could take it and dish it out, too. She certainly kept them on their toes. He gave her a mock-hurt look.

"Hey, I picked that paint out. It was a sunny shade of yellow."

Becca sputtered with laughter. "It sure was sunny. You would have had to wear sunglasses inside the house. You might have burned your corneas."

Travis cracked up. "She's right, babe. The paint was horrendous. We could use it to paint highway guardrails, though. No one will miss them for sure."

"Okay, I won't be picking out paint any longer. In fact, I vote that you and Becca pick out the color scheme for the house going forward."

Travis snorted. "That was a given. You are officially fired from interior-decorating duties. From now on you're the muscle around here."

Mark struck a pose, flexing his biceps. "About time I was appreciated for my brawn."

Travis pulled him into his arms and gave him a kiss. "I've always appreciated your physique. Becca, what do you think about our Mark's body?"

Becca's face went pink, and she seemed frozen for a moment with shock. Mark almost told her to ignore Travis's teasing when she answered.

"I think I'd like to run my hands all over it."

Becca's voice was soft but sure. Travis gave Mark a triumphant smile as he stepped back.

"Then come here and help yourself. I know Mark wants it, and I want to watch you."

Becca stood up and crossed the few steps to where Mark stood. He held his breath as her warm hands caressed his own before sliding up his arms. Her soft fingers explored his biceps, up over his shoulders, and down his chest to his stomach. He could feel his ab muscles tensing under her hands and his cock hardening in anticipation. He wanted to beg her to move her hands further south, but his mouth had suddenly gone dry. Travis's voice, however, was working perfectly.

"Go ahead and let your fingers touch his cock, sweetie. He wants it so bad. We've dreamed about your hands on us."

* * * *

With Cassie and Jillian's exhortations in her mind, Becca didn't hesitate to let her fingers slide down his ridged, flat stomach to stroke the bulge in his jeans. She explored his hardness, marveling at his length and girth. He was impressive in size. Cream dripped from her pussy in anticipation. She couldn't wait to feel his hard cock pounding her to ecstasy.

"That feels so fucking good."

Mark's voice came out as a groan. With a half smile, she popped open his button fly one by one, teasing him with soft brushes. She fell to her knees while her hand slipped under his boxer shorts to encircle him. Her other hand gripped his muscular thigh as she pulled his cock free. The reddish-purple mushroom head was already dripping pre-cum, and Becca licked her lips, dying to get a taste. Travis stroked her hair.

"Do you like sucking cock, sweetie? You've got two horny men here who love giving and getting head."

Becca pulled Mark's jeans down around his thighs and began to kiss her way to the crinkly sac already pulling tight.

"I've never had much luck with oral sex, but I want to suck you and Mark so much."

Mark's chuckle was lost in a moan as her tongue swept around his balls.

"I think you're about to have a turnaround in luck with us, baby. I've been dreaming about eating your sweet pussy for months now."

Becca watched, fascinated, as Travis turned Mark's head toward him and captured his lips in a long kiss. She had thought she might feel strange or out of place watching the two of them, but she only felt lust. It was hot watching them together. Arousal curled in her belly, sending arrows of pleasure to her cunt.

"Does Becca's mouth feel good, babe?"

"Fuck, yeah. It's like having a hot glove surrounding my dick."

Mark tugged at her hair, and Becca obliged him by engulfing the head of his cock in her waiting mouth. She began to suck and lick his shaft before letting it pop out of her mouth and swirling her tongue around the head and up and down his velvety length. She was so lost in the feel and taste of him she was startled when a tongue joined her own.

Travis had dropped to his knees and was running his tongue along the veins in Mark's dick. Mark was moaning and groaning as their two tongues sent him closer and closer to the edge. Becca's tongue tangled with Travis's as they lapped at the sweet pre-cum leaking from Mark's cock. Travis pulled her close and their tongues rubbed against each other in a hot, sweaty kiss. Travis's hands were cupping her breasts, rubbing his thumbs over her already-hard and pointed nipples. She whimpered in frustration as she pressed closer to his warm body. She wanted their clothes gone and to feel flesh on flesh.

Her hands started tugging at Travis's T-shirt, and he chuckled before pulling away just slightly to look into her eyes.

"We want you, Becca. Do you want us? Are you ready for us?"

Becca threw up her hands in frustration.

"You have to ask? I'm on my knees with a cock in my mouth and your tongue in it, too, trying to wrestle your clothes off. Are these the actions of a woman who's not sure what she wants? Let me make it clear then. I want you and Mark to fuck me. Hard. Fast. I want your tongues in my pussy and your cocks there, too. Is that clear enough?"

Becca almost laughed at Travis's shocked expression. She glanced up, and Mark had almost the exact same expression.

Travis ran his hands through his hair. "Uh, yeah, that's pretty clear, sweetie. You've got a mouth on you, that's for sure. Mark and I thought we might have to tone things down in the bedroom for you, but shit, you might have to tone things down for us. Go easy on us, baby. We're just men."

Becca was incredulous as she struggled to her feet.

"Tone things down? I'm not a virgin, for heaven's sake. You can thank Wiley James our junior year of high school for that. I'm not completely innocent, either. This is a ménage town, guys. Women talk. I had a pretty good idea what I would be getting into. And I have some ideas of my own, too."

Travis grinned as he stood up. "I wouldn't mind hearing those. How about you, babe?"

Mark grinned, too. "Hell, yeah. If we're sharing ideas, I've got this one where you're fucking Becca and I'm fucking you."

Becca's arousal soared as the visual took shape in her brain.

She nodded. "I'm totally on board with that idea."

Mark shook his head. "You're a lot younger than us. We thought you might be kind of sheltered and, well, innocent."

She didn't want to mock them but just couldn't stop herself.

"A prim, proper lady who never cusses or has sex?"

They had the grace to look a little ashamed. Becca shoved at Mark's shoulder.

"You can't stay too damn innocent in a small town. Hell, just the stories of what my brothers got into would have curled my hair. The girl next door I'm not."

Travis grimaced. "Apparently. We didn't mean to assume anything. We just wanted to be sensitive."

"I know, and I appreciate that. I may not be the girl next door, but I am something else. A woman. I want you to treat me like the grown woman I am. Can you do that?"

Both men nodded vigorously. Mark ran his hands down her arm, sending sparks straight to her clit.

"Can we treat you like a woman right now?"

Becca crossed her arms over her chest and gave them a stern look. "You damn well better. You've got me all hot and bothered here."

Mark pulled up his pants. "It is our fault. But don't get too cocky, sweetheart. This guy is always in charge in the bedroom."

Mark pointed to Travis, whose expression had changed from one of shame to passion. He was definitely going to make love to her.

Becca turned to Travis. "You're dominant in the bedroom?"

Travis gave her a look that let her know without any doubt the answer to her question.

"Yes. How dominant I am will be up to you, of course. But I like to be in charge."

Becca nodded. "Fine. Then get this show on the road."

Travis pointed to the hallway. The bedrooms were down that hall.

"Everyone get in the master bedroom and get naked. Now."

* * * *

Travis hid a grin as Mark and Becca headed for the bedroom. By the time he arrived, Mark had already pulled his paint-spotted T-shirt off and was pushing his jeans down his muscular thighs. Travis felt the familiar stirrings seeing the man he loved. His arousal was so much more this time because his sweet Becca was helping Mark tug those jeans off.

Becca was turning out to be a surprise in the bedroom. Outside of it, she was sweet and loving, with just a touch of smart aleck. She was resilient and had strong beliefs about helping others. To find out she was a woman who embraced her sexuality was the ultimate aphrodisiac to Travis. She was someone he could easily fall in love with. Hell, he had been halfway there already even before today. This would probably complete his head-over-heels tumble. His naturally cautious nature was nowhere to be seen.

He gave Becca a scowl. "You are still dressed."

She gave him a pretty pout, running her finger down his chest, leaving a line of heat where she had touched him.

"Mark's naked, though." She smiled coyly. "I helped."

Damn, she was hot. His blood was pounding in his ears just from her teasing, and his cock was as hard as concrete. He wanted to test just how open she really was about sex.

"Look at Mark. Tell me what you see."

Her eyes lit up at his challenge. She walked a few circles around Mark, taking him in from every angle.

"I see an incredibly sexy man. He's handsome, too, with his blond hair and square jaw. I love the new goatee. I can't wait for it to tickle my cunt. His shoulders are wide and his chest is muscular. God, his abs are so flat and you can count his six-pack."

Her fingers explored the ridges of Mark's stomach. Travis was itching to feel her fingers on his own body.

"His legs are strong and defined. His ass is spectacular. It makes me want to take a bite out of it."

"Go ahead. Mark, stand there and let Becca do as she pleases with your body."

Mark grinned and spread his arms wide. "Be my guest, baby."

Becca gave him an evil look and licked her lips before dropping to her knees. Her hands caressed Mark's firm buttocks before her eyes locked with Travis's. She leaned forward and let her teeth sink into his ass muscles. Mark's cock jumped in excitement. Travis knew she hadn't bitten Mark hard, but she had definitely received a reaction.

Mark groaned. "Again, fuck, again."

Becca lifted her lips and bit down onto the other cheek. Travis could see she was using her tongue and sucking at the taut skin. Mark had his eyes closed in ecstasy.

"Is there anywhere else you want to bite Mark? He looks like he's enjoying it."

Becca shook her head then changed her mind and nodded. "His chest."

"Go ahead. His body is yours to torture."

Becca repeated the ritual on Mark's pectorals. Each time, Mark's cock would jump and a groan would be ripped from his throat. Travis knew Mark was getting close. Whether Becca had figured it out or not, Mark liked it rough. She was giving him exactly what he wanted. Mark was shaking with pleasure, his eyes glazed with passion.

"Undress now. I want Mark to see and explore your body."

Chapter 7

Becca tugged her shirt over her head with shaking hands. The sex play so far had been raunchy and hot. She had never bitten anyone during sex before, but Mark had seemed to enjoy it. Travis had obviously enjoyed watching. He had a tent in his jeans that made her mouth water. Hopefully, she'd get him in her mouth before too long.

She was feeling completely enveloped in the relationship, not like an outsider. Watching them together had been unbelievably hot, too. She hoped she could convince them to have sex while she watched.

She tossed her old T-shirt aside and pushed her worn cutoff jeans down her legs. She tossed them on top of her shirt. She stood before Travis and Mark in her white lace panties and bra. She had purchased all-new underwear since they moved to town.

Travis looked at Mark. "She seems shy. Help her with the rest."

Mark gave her a lazy smile. "Travis is probably going to want to punish you for not following his directions and getting undressed."

He reached behind her and her bra came apart with a pinch of his fingers. He pulled it down her arms, and it joined the growing pile of clothes. He dropped to his knees and tugged her panties down her legs, kissing each inch of skin from the tops of her thighs to the toes of her feet. Honey dripped from her pussy and it clenched with need. She wanted a cock inside of her.

She was finally naked, her body bare to their gazes. She normally would have felt self-conscious. She had ample curves and her stomach was not quite flat. She had been one of the first of her friends to need a bra and had always been a little embarrassed about her D cups. The hungry light in their eyes kept her from covering herself with her hands. They liked what they were seeing, and she reveled in the feeling of being so wanted. It had been a long time since a man had lusted after her. Today she had two.

Mark whistled. "Holy fuck, Trav. Take a look at those tits. I can't wait to get those babies in my mouth. And have you ever seen anything more gorgeous than her round ass? We're going to love spanking and fucking it."

Mark ran his hands through her long hair, tugging her head back so she was looking directly into his blue eyes.

"How does that sound to you, pretty girl? Would you like Trav and me to spank and fuck your fantastic ass?"

Becca swallowed the lump in her throat. She had finally met men who could give her what she needed.

"So far, you both seem to be mostly talk. Fun, dirty talk, but all talk nonetheless."

Travis's eyes narrowed. Shit, she was in trouble.

"Take our little princess over to the bed, babe. I want her legs spread wide. We're going to lick her creamy pussy until she screams our names."

Becca felt her knees go weak. Luckily, Mark scooped her up into his arms and was carrying her to the king-size bed.

"Wait! I'm too heavy to carry."

Mark just laughed and dropped her on the mattress.

"Hardly. You're just a tiny thing."

Becca pushed herself up to the top of the bed, leaning back against the dark oak headboard. The men were looking at her like she was a banquet and they hadn't eaten in weeks. Travis stood at the foot of the bed, devouring her with his eyes.

"Spread your legs, sweetheart. Show us how much you want to have your pussy licked."

Now wasn't the time to chicken out. She desperately wanted their tongues in her cunt. She spread her legs wide, her pussy completely on display. Mark practically growled his arousal as he dove in tongue first. He lapped at her clit lightly before running his tongue through the folds and down to her opening. He tongue-fucked her while Travis watched with glowing, hot eyes. Mark lifted his head.

"You've got to taste her pussy, Trav. It's so sweet and spicy. I'm going to eat her pussy every single day."

Mark moved to the side, and Travis took his place. He never said a word but simply held her gaze with his. Even as he lowered his head to swipe his tongue from clit to opening, he never lost eye contact. Becca half screamed at the sensations.

Mark chuckled. "I think she likes it, but she's not screaming our names yet. Keep licking while I worship her gorgeous breasts."

Travis went back to work on her dripping cunt. His tongue was a tool of pleasure and torture. It seemed to lick everywhere but where she needed it most—directly on her clit. She tried to wriggle her clit under his tongue, but he had her firmly pinned to the bed with a hand on the inside of each thigh. With Mark leaning over her torso, starting to lap at her nipples, she was effectively their prisoner, albeit a willing one.

Mark sucked her already-tight nipple into his mouth and slid his teeth lightly across the sensitive flesh. Becca moaned and arched her back, wanting and needing more. He repeated the process on her other nipple while pinching the neglected one. She would have come off the bed if she hadn't been held down so firmly. Travis lifted his head.

"Her nipples are very sensitive. We'll have to buy some clamps for her. She'll love those."

Becca groaned at the thought of tight clamps on her breasts. She had fantasized about them since Cassie had told a story about them at one of their Monday-night dinners.

Mark laughed. "I think she likes the idea. I don't have any clamps, but let's see if we can pretend."

Just as Mark's teeth clamped down on her nipple, Travis slipped a finger inside her clenching pussy. She tightened her muscles around him as he moved his finger in and out before adding a second. He swirled his fingers and found her sweet spot. He rubbed the swollen flesh and closed his mouth over her clit.

Mark paused in worrying her nipple with his teeth. "Time to come, baby. Come for me and Trav."

She couldn't have stopped if she wanted to. Her climax came over her like a tidal wave, strong and unforgiving. It seemed to lift her from the bed and throw her back down. She felt her body go taut, and then wave after wave tore through her. She fought for breath and then let go, the pleasure running over her until she was wrung out. Her eyes fluttered open to see her two handsome men with triumphant grins.

Her mouth twisted into a wry smile. "Feeling very proud of yourself, aren't you? What do you have planned for act two?"

Travis leaned over her and kissed her, letting his tongue sweep over hers. She tasted herself and then tasted only him. She pulled him closer and let her hands twist in his silky brown hair. She protested when he broke the kiss to pull open the nightstand.

"Act two is going to be you getting a good, hard fucking from me and Mark."

Oh, goody. Bring it on.

* * * *

Travis snagged two condoms from the bedside table and threw one to Mark. He handed his to Becca and then hopped off the bed, pulling his shirt over his head.

"Mark and I have been together for years and don't use these with each other, but we didn't want to assume anything with you."

Becca levered up on her elbows watching Travis shuck his clothes.

"I'm not on the pill. I haven't had any reason to be on it for quite a while. I had my yearly exam in January. I don't have any diseases."

Mark gave her a smile. "We just want you to feel comfortable. Trav and I have always used condoms with anyone but each other. We've been tested and we're clean. If you're not on the pill, we'll use the condoms."

Travis pushed his boxer shorts down, and Becca drank in the sight of his muscled body and impressive cock. He wasn't as tan as Mark nor as lean. His torso was wide and his stomach just as flat. His arms were huge and his thighs massive. She vaguely remembered them saying Travis liked to ride his bike. His cock was thick and long with a slight curve. It was beefier than Mark's, and she gulped, wondering what it would feel like inside her. Mark's cock had appeared daunting enough. She hadn't been with anyone in quite a while.

"Uh, guys, I haven't done this in a while, and you are, well…"

Travis plucked the condom packet from her fingers and tore it open with his teeth.

"I'll take it slow, honey. We'll fit just fine."

Travis leaned over her and brushed his lips lightly against hers. She was undone by the tender look on his face. His dominant nature was still apparent but was wrapped up in so much care and gentleness she couldn't be fearful. Instead, she relaxed and let him take control, safe in the knowledge he would indeed take care of her.

His condom-covered cock brushed at her entrance. She was wet and ready, but he took his time, rubbing the head from opening to clit as he licked and nipped at her sensitive nipples.

"Travis, oh please, fuck me! I need you now!"

Their eyes met and held as he slowly pushed his cock inside her. He was big, and for a moment her muscles didn't want to give way. He paused and let her exhale and consciously relax. His face was a taut mask of control, and he began pushing forward again. She was drenched with cream and his cock now slid in easily. He held her gaze as he thrust in to the hilt. He stopped, letting her body get used to his invasion. Pleasure curled inside her and arousal built at being this full of cock. Her body was screaming to move. She raked her fingernails down his muscled back.

He began to move, slowly at first. He pulled almost all the way out then slammed back home, sending frissons of pleasure through her belly, cunt, and clit. She dug her heels into the mattress and met each thrust with her pelvis, loving the way he rubbed her clit each time. Soon they were panting and groaning as their bodies found the rhythm they both needed.

"Come for me, baby."

Travis's hand reached between them, rubbing small circles around her swollen and sensitive clit. It only took a moment and she was flying apart. Her cunt clamped down on his cock and she was shaking with the intensity of her orgasm. He thrust one last time inside her before tensing. The veins on his neck stood out and he gritted his teeth. He muttered a filthy word, and then she could feel his cock jerking inside of her. It sent minishudders through her pussy, leaving her breathless.

He lay on her for a moment before pulling reluctantly from her. He gave her a last tender kiss before turning her over to Mark. Travis disappeared into the bathroom, and Mark began running his hands all over her already-sensitized skin. It made her shudder with pleasure, and he chuckled softly in her ear.

"I don't think it will take much more to send you over again, will it, sweetie?"

* * * *

Mark's cock was hard enough to pound nails. Between her teasing foreplay and gentle biting from earlier, then watching Travis fuck her into oblivion, he knew he wouldn't last long. Perhaps he should give her the reins this time. It might cool him down a little. He stretched out on the bed and patted his stomach.

"You're in control of this one. Saddle up and ride, baby."

To his surprise, Becca didn't seem enthused.

"Well, I've just never been very good at being on top. I never seem to know what to do."

So their seductress did have a few things she was unsure about. *Time to take those insecurities away.*

"No way to do it wrong. Do whatever you want, and I'll lie here and enjoy it. Deal?"

Becca looked doubtful but swung her leg over his hips anyway. She looked so beautiful. Her golden hair was in disarray, her lips swollen, and her creamy skin had pink marks on her breasts and thighs from their whiskers. They just had to make this work between the three of them. He couldn't imagine not having this in his life.

She lowered herself slowly on his condom-covered cock. He longed for the day when he wouldn't have to suit up. He dreamily pictured a little girl with Becca's golden hair and blue eyes or a little boy with Travis's brown hair and golden-brown eyes.

Her pussy hugged his cock tightly, and he hissed in pleasure as she seated herself fully.

"Aw, fuck, baby, you feel so damn good."

Becca started to move, jerkily at first then with more confidence. He held himself very still while she found the rhythm and tempo she needed. It wasn't long before she was bouncing up and down on him, her hands braced on his chest. He was lost in the pleasure of her hot, wet cunt surrounding him, the smell of her shampoo and arousal, when he heard a loud smack and Becca's expression turned to surprise then passion.

Travis had come up behind her and had smacked her ass cheek smartly.

"This spanking is for not getting undressed when I told you to. Keep riding him and take your punishment like a good girl."

It was as if someone had lit a fire inside of her. Every time she came down on him, thrusting his cock deep in her pussy, Travis would spank her ass cheek. Becca's pussy had clamped down on his hard cock and she was grinding her clit on his groin, moaning and arching her back. She wanted more spanking and she wanted more cock.

They gave it to her.

She rode Mark hard and fast and then finally screamed their names as she froze above him. Travis kept spanking her but faster and more lightly. The expression on his face and on Becca's sent Mark over the edge, too. He grabbed her hips and groaned as his hot cum shot into the condom. It felt like his balls were turned inside out as the pleasure went on for long moments. He finally fell still under her, feeling sated. At least for now. He knew he would always want this woman who had collapsed on his chest in exhaustion. She was amazing. He looked over her shoulder at Travis.

Travis had a wondrous look on his face. Mark knew it had never been like this for them with anyone else, and it never would. This was the woman they had been waiting for. Fifteen years had been a long time but more than worth it. She was their third. Mark felt complete as he gazed at the man he had loved for so many years. He reached out and brought Travis's fingers to his lips.

I love you. So much.

Chapter 8

Becca was hungrier than she ever remembered being in her life. They had fallen asleep after the most amazing sex of her life. She had been sandwiched between their hard bodies, surrounded by their warmth and their scent. She had never felt so safe and cared for.

When they woke, she thought it might be awkward, but their loving, teasing manner put her at ease. She couldn't regret what they had done, and they made it clear it had been as earth shattering for them, too.

They had showered and changed then driven her to her condo so she could do the same. Mark and Travis had insisted they take her out on the date they had been planning all week. She was now sitting in the diner with her men, smelling the food and feeling happy and content. She perused the menu. Travis pulled her menu down to get her attention.

"What do you recommend? We're still pretty new in town."

Becca pursed her lips in thought.

"Saturday's special is the lasagna, which is awesome. They serve it with bread dripping in garlic butter."

Becca's stomach growled angrily. Mark shook his head.

"We haven't done a very good job today."

Her face turned a little pink as she gave them a flirtatious look.

"I don't know about that. You guys were very good today."

Mark chuckled. "I meant we didn't do a very good job of taking care of you. We should have fed you earlier."

"We were busy earlier, and then we fell asleep. Exhausted."

Mark threw an arm around her. "Happily busy and exhausted, baby. But we need to make sure we take care of you all the time, not just in bed."

Becca shoved at his chest. "I can take care of myself. I'm not the innocent girl next door, remember?"

Travis shot her a heated look. "We remember quite well."

The bell over the door rang and Cassie, Zach, and Chase entered the diner talking and laughing. Cassie's face lit up when she saw Becca. Becca waved her over.

"I didn't expect to see you here tonight. I thought you were trying out the new tandoori chicken recipe."

Cassie grimaced. "Tried and failed. It was awful. Truly bad. We threw it in the trash and headed straight here. We're going to bingo tonight anyway."

Cassie looked her over carefully, and Becca felt her face flame. Cassie gave her a knowing smile before turning to the men.

"So, what have you been up to today? You all look…exhausted."

Travis grinned. "Painting."

Zach laughed. "You convinced Becca to help you paint? You owe her a meal then."

Mark leaned back and threw his arm across Becca's shoulders.

"Becca did a great job painting. The living room and dining room look really good. She even picked out the color. Why don't you pull that table over and join us? We haven't even ordered yet."

Chase pulled a chair out for Cassie while Zach pulled the table over to theirs.

"Don't mind if we do. We're all starved."

Cassie looked so happy with her men. Becca felt her heart squeeze as Zach lifted Cassie's fingers to his lips for a kiss. He kissed each one, lingering longer on the finger that held the diamond engagement ring they had given her on Thanksgiving Day along with a golden retriever puppy she had named Duffy. Cassie was Zach and Chase's whole world. What would it feel like to be the center of someone's life?

Mark seemed to be in tune with her thoughts. He pulled her closer and dropped a kiss on top of her head. She turned to give him a smile. He was so handsome. She let her fingers trace his freshly shaven jaw. Chase cleared his throat with a grin.

"Good thing Jack and Ryan aren't here to watch this."

Zach elbowed his brother. "Quit it. Becca's a grown woman. It's not any of Ryan and Jack's business. I'm guessing they've got their hands full with Jillian anyway."

Becca nodded in agreement. "They don't need to know my business."

Travis put down his menu with a serious expression.

"Actually, we talked to your brothers at the poker game Monday night. They seem fine with us dating you."

Becca felt anger bubble in her empty stomach.

"You talked to my brothers about our business. Why?"

* * * *

Mark tried to soothe his obviously upset woman.

"They were being good brothers and concerned about our intentions. We assured them our intentions were honorable. They seemed fine after that."

Becca slapped the table and her eyes sparkled.

"It's none of their damn business. I don't like you discussing our relationship with people outside of it. What would you have done if they weren't okay with it? Would you have backed off? Not given me a choice as if I couldn't make a flipping decision for myself?"

Mark was taken aback by Becca's anger. He figured there was probably more going on here.

"Of course you can make your own decisions. They were concerned, that's all. We won't discuss our relationship with them ever again. We apologize if we've upset you. It was never our intention."

Travis grabbed her hand.

"I apologize also. We just wanted to have your brothers on our side. I guess we thought it would help. We would not have backed off. We made it clear we want to be with you. If your brothers weren't okay with it, we would have been sad about that, but ultimately it was your decision. Please accept our apologies."

Becca seemed somewhat mollified.

"My brothers have been under the impression for years that I am not capable of running my own life. I don't want to get involved with two men who feel the same way."

"We don't feel the same way," Travis assured her.

Cassie and her men had been watching their exchange with interest. Cassie finally lifted her menu and changed the subject.

"So what's everyone going to order? I think I'll get the lasagna."

Mark exhaled in relief as Becca relaxed next to him and chatted with Cassie about the merits of the diner's garlic bread versus Charlie's. They would need to tread lightly around Becca and the subject of her brothers. There was definitely some history there they needed to find out.

* * * *

After a sudden downpour, Becca had suggested heading to the firehouse for bingo with Cassie, Zach, and Chase instead of the drive-in. The firehouse was lit up and packed with what seemed like the entire town.

Cassie pulled Travis aside during the break. "I think you need to understand what happened at the diner."

Travis felt relief and gratitude. He hadn't been sure why Becca was so angry, but he knew it was more than them seeking her brothers' blessing.

"You just need to understand that Becca has lived in Ryan's and Jack's shadows pretty much her whole life. She was always their cute little sister. People haven't taken her very seriously. She does a lot of work in the community and runs her own business, but she's still Ryan and Jack's little sister. Compound that with Ryan and Jack being so overprotective since they lost their mom, and you have a recipe for one frustrated woman. A grown woman who wants respect for the things she's accomplished. She wants people to realize she can stand on her own two feet and make her own decisions."

Travis rubbed his jaw in frustration. "I can't make an entire community change their minds about her."

Cassie shook her head. "You don't have to, Travis. All she really needs is respect from you and Mark. She's scared, you know."

"Scared of what? Us?"

"She's scared of not being an equal partner in this relationship. She said she didn't want to be a *chew toy* for you two."

"A *chew toy*, for fuck's sake. She's not a chew toy. We're falling in love with her, Cass."

Cassie nodded. "I can see that. But you need to make sure she feels like she's a part of things. She wants to be treated like a grown woman. Be sure to ask her thoughts and opinions. Respect them. It might be easy to fall back onto old habits with just the two of you making all the decisions."

"Thanks, Cass. We'll take care of this. I promise."

Cassie headed back to her men. "See that you do. I'm told the woman is always the center of a ménage relationship. Make her feel that way and she'll fall in love with you."

Travis headed to find Mark. He needed to make sure they were on the same page. They would sweep all doubts from their woman's mind.

* * * *

Becca spied her brothers talking outside during the break from bingo. She'd been wanting to rip them a new asshole since hearing about their little discussion with Mark and Travis on Monday night. She was tired of her brothers acting like she was some dumb blonde. Time to remind them she was a big girl who could take care of herself.

"I'm glad to find you two together. I want to talk to both of you."

Ryan gave her a big smile and a hug.

"Hey there, little sis, any luck at bingo tonight?"

Jack gave her a quick hug, took one look at her stormy expression, and headed for the door to the fire station.

"Nice to see you, baby girl, but I've got to—"

Becca grabbed his arm. "Stop right there, Jack. I've got a few words to say to you. Both of you, actually."

Ryan pushed himself away from the stair railing where he had been leaning.

"You look pretty pissed, sis. What did we do this time?"

Becca had had a few hours to work up a full head of steam. She was going to hit her dear brothers with both barrels. She shook her finger at them.

"First of all, I'm not a baby girl. I'm twenty-fucking-six. A grown woman by any society's standards. Jack, you're only a few years older. I'm tired of this overprotective stuff. It has to stop. Now."

Ryan looked shocked. "What overprotective stuff? We haven't done anything."

Becca put her hands on her hips. "Oh really? Are you sure? What about Monday night?"

Ryan looked puzzled, and then red stained his cheeks. Jack was checking out his own shoelaces.

"So? You do remember Monday, don't you? I believe you asked Mark and Travis their intentions? Who gave you the right to do that?"

Ryan always felt a good defense was a good offense.

"We're your older brothers. We care about you. We just want to make sure you don't get hurt. I think we have a right to care about you."

Becca nodded, her stomach churning. She usually backed down to Ryan at this point. She couldn't today. She needed them to understand how important this was to her.

"Yes, you do. What you don't have is the right to interfere. What if their intentions aren't honorable? What if they just want a piece of ass?"

Jack's head flew up. "Now watch your mouth—"

Becca got in Jack's face. "I will not. You don't watch your mouth, so why should I? I didn't get in Jillian's face about her intentions, and Mark and Travis didn't get in your face about yours. This is nothing but double-standard bullshit. It's okay for my brothers to have sex, but not me. Right?"

"Shit, we know that, and we apologized to them about it. We just want to protect you, that's all. And as for having sex, we're your brothers and we sure as shit don't want to hear about you having a sex life."

Becca rolled her eyes. "It's okay for me to hear you having wild, screaming sex with Jillian in my own home, but you can't stomach the thought that I might be having sex with Mark and Travis. Well, here's a newsflash, boys. I am having sex with Mark and Travis. Great, awesome sex. And do you know why? Because I am an adult and I want to. I don't know if I'll marry these guys, but I want to be with them. This is none of your business and not up for discussion. Do I make myself clear?"

Ryan's face was red with embarrassment and anger. "Crystal. Excuse the hell out of me for giving a damn about my sister's happiness. It sure as hell won't happen ever again."

Ryan stomped back into the firehouse to join Zach and Chase, leaving Becca with Jack.

"Let him cool off, sis. You know how he is. I will give you props, though. He rarely loses his cool. Usually it's me blowing a gasket."

Becca grimaced. "I wasn't trying to piss him off. You both just need to back the fuck off of my life."

Jackson nodded. "I got it. You have a point, and we were out of line. When Ryan cools down he'll agree. You know, we did a pretty good job raising you. You turned out pretty good."

Becca linked her arm with his. "You didn't raise me. Mom and Dad did. And hell yes, they did a good job. With all of us."

They headed into the firehouse arm in arm.

"Give Ryan a day or two, sis. He'll be groveling for forgiveness."

Chapter 9

Jillian caught Becca as she was heading out the door of the firehouse with Mark and Travis.

"I don't suppose you know why Ryan stomped out of here muttering under his breath, do you?"

Becca nodded. "Was he walking funny, too? Because I ripped him a new one. I'm sorry that you're going to have to deal with him tonight, Jillian, but he needed to hear what I had to say."

Mark look concerned. "What did you say to him, sweetheart?"

"That it was none of his damn business who I slept with and if it was serious or not. He won't bother you guys again."

Jillian rolled her eyes and laughed. "Oh, it's going to be fun tonight. Ryan was breathing fire when he left. I'll just have to channel all that energy into something more fun."

Jillian had a naughty look on her face. Mark grimaced.

"And now we know how Ryan felt tonight. We don't want to hear about you putting the moves on your fiancé."

Becca rounded on Mark. "You're such hypocrites. You want to have sex yourselves, but you don't want *girls* to have sex."

Travis held up his hands in surrender. "Now wait a minute, baby. Yes, we like sex, and yes, we like to have sex. With girls. With you. It's not just Jillian we don't want to hear about. I, personally, don't want to hear about Cassie's sex life or anyone else's for that matter."

He took some of the wind out of Becca's sails. She really didn't want to be mad, but she needed to make her point.

"Good girls have sex. We like it, too. A lot."

Jillian raised her hand. "I'll second that."

Cassie joined the group. "What are we voting on?"

Jillian grinned. "Whether we like sex."

Cassie gave her men across the room a long look. "Hell, yeah."

Travis groaned. "Becca, honey, can we go home now? I don't think this conversation is headed in any direction we want to go."

Becca agreed. She was being evil to Mark and Travis because she was pissed at Ryan and Jack.

"Yes, take me home. I don't want to argue with Ryan again, and I really don't want to argue with you, either."

Her boys looked relieved, and Jillian held her back for just a moment.

"Give them hell, Becca. Don't let them get away with that good-girl crap."

* * * *

Becca pushed open the door of her condo and flipped on the lights. It had been a quiet ride back from bingo, and she knew it was her fault. She shouldn't have let her annoyance with Ryan and Jack interfere with her first real date with Mark and Travis.

It had been a wonderful day. Her body still tingled from their lovemaking earlier. She wanted to be with them again but didn't want to appear too forward. They were hanging by the open front door, looking unsure.

"Do you want to come in? I'm really sorry things got hairy toward the end there. I was mad at Ryan and Jack, not you."

They both looked relieved and closed the front door. Travis wrapped his arms around her and pulled her close.

"It's okay, sweetheart. Ryan and Travis are just protective of you. They know you're grown up, but old habits die hard. Wouldn't the opposite be worse?"

Becca sighed and laid her head on his chest. She could smell his manly scent and feel his heart beating under her cheek.

"Yes, it would. I just want people to treat me like an adult. But I guess I maybe didn't act like one tonight. Damn."

Mark came up behind her and kissed her neck softly.

"You're allowed to be mad. Just, please, let us know if you're mad at us. We'll talk and work it out. And by the way, we know that good girls like sex, and boy, are we damn glad about that."

Becca chuckled and let her head fall back on Mark's chest, feeling his warmth.

"That would be the grown-up thing to do. I hate being called a good girl, you know."

Travis frowned. "Why? What's wrong with being a good girl?"

Becca thought for a moment. "It sounds so simplistic, so uncomplicated, so bland. Ryan was the cool, responsible one, Jack was the passionate, spontaneous one. And me. I was the good girl. It was boring, unexciting, and it made me practically invisible. Who wants to be invisible?"

She felt Mark's breath tickle her neck.

"You're not invisible to us. We think you're exciting as hell, too. Can't you tell?"

Mark pressed his groin into her backside, and she could feel his hard cock. She reached back and ran her hand along his button fly. She hummed with pleasure.

"I can tell. You must think I'm pretty exciting. This cock feels very hard."

Travis pressed closer so she could feel his cock against her belly.

"I'm hard as a rock, too, baby. Is our bad girl going to do anything about it?"

Becca gave them a slow smile. "Oh hell yeah, I'm gonna do something about it."

She pulled away and headed to the bedroom.

"Let's get naked and let me show you just how good and bad I can be."

* * * *

Mark followed Becca into her bedroom. His heart was pounding, his palms were sweaty, and his cock was rock hard. He had all the signs. The signs of falling in love. Travis pulled the covers down on the bed and fell back with a loud sigh.

"Damn, that feels good. Seems like we've been on the go since dawn."

Becca laughed and started unzipping her jeans.

"That's because we have. We can just sleep if you want."

She had a very innocent look on her face, but Mark knew she had the dirty mind to go with it. He was never too tired.

"Trav can go to sleep if he wants, but I won't leave you hanging. I'm never too tired to make love to my woman."

Travis levered up on his elbows. "I'm not, either. I was just saying it's been a long day and getting horizontal will feel good. Really, really good."

Travis patted the mattress next to him as Becca tossed her jeans aside and pulled her shirt over her head. She had on baby-pink panties and a lace bra to match. Her hard nipples were clearly outlined and beckoning to his lips. He couldn't wait to worship her.

Travis reached up and tugged her down on the bed, rolling her under him and nibbling on the sensitive skin of her neck. He started traveling down her body, planting openmouthed kisses on her creamy skin while tugging the remainder of her clothes off. Mark stretched out on her other side and cupped her bared breasts in his hands. They were perfect. Generous and round, with nipples the color of berries.

He licked at each of them and watched them crinkle tighter before rubbing his goatee across their sensitized surface. Becca wriggled but pulled his head down to anchor his face to her chest. She needn't have bothered. He wasn't going anywhere anytime soon.

He licked, sucked, and nipped her nipples and all around her breasts. He ran his tongue down the valley between her breasts, all the way to her belly button. He nipped at it with his teeth. She was moaning and panting the whole time, entreating them to lick her, suck her, anything, just make her come. Mark loved her unabashed responses to their lovemaking. The town might think of her as a simple good girl, but she was a woman. A woman who reveled in her sexuality. He and Travis were lucky men.

He watched as Travis spread her legs wide and lowered his head, licking her from anus to clit. Becca screamed Travis's name as her head fell back and her eyes closed in pleasure. Hot damn, his woman was a screamer.

"Make her scream some more, Trav. Let's wake up the neighbors giving our woman pleasure."

* * * *

She had just screamed so loudly they probably heard her at the firehouse.

That'll change my good-girl image in a hurry.

Travis was teasing her pussy with butterfly-light licks. She wound her fingers in his hair and tried to tug his head where she wanted it, but Mark just chuckled and pulled her hands up over her head, anchoring them there. The thought of being restrained and helpless to their mouths and hands sent her arousal soaring and honey dripping from her pussy.

"She likes that, Mark. We'll need to get some silk rope to restrain her."

She felt Mark's breath in her ear.

"Do you like being restrained, baby? Do you like being at our mercy?"

She would have answered, but she was beyond words. She could only nod as Travis ate at her pussy, devouring her cream. She could hear his whispered words of praise. He loved her taste, her aroma, the feel of her cunt when he pressed two fingers inside her.

Mark started sucking her already-sensitive nipples again, and she went into sensory overload. The pleasure was too much. She couldn't hold back the floodgates as she screamed their names again and again. Cream poured from her cunt and her pussy clenched, wanting a cock to fill it, fuck it. She felt the pleasure roll through her and saw dancing lights before slumping on the bed, wrung out from her climax.

Their hands stroked her skin, sending tingles of pleasure through her. She heard their murmured words but couldn't make out what they were saying. It didn't matter as the words were tender to go along with their caresses.

She caught their hands under hers.

"I think I need to return the favor. That was amazing. Awesome. You know, all those *A* words."

Mark chuckled and began to nuzzle her neck.

"I could go for awesome. How about you, Trav?"

Travis was stretched out on Becca's other side, stroking her stomach.

"Awesome sounds good to me. One good, hard fucking coming up, pretty girl. It's our turn."

* * * *

Travis helped Becca get into position on the pillows, her golden-blonde hair messy and tangled. Her lips were swollen from their kisses, and her skin was fragrant and soft. Such a contrast to when he and Mark made love. He had the best of both worlds in his arms. He pulled Mark close for a hot kiss, their tongues tangling together. This man still sent him into overdrive. He knew exactly what he wanted to do tonight.

"Mark, grab the lube. I want you to fuck me while I fuck Becca."

Becca's eyes widened, but her surprise didn't deter him. If she wanted to be an equal, an integral part of their relationship, there was no time like the present.

He rolled on a condom and positioned himself between her legs, rubbing the head of his cock up and down her drenched slit. She arched and moaned, clutching at his shoulders.

"Fuck me, Travis. Fuck me."

Travis captured her lips with his own, drinking in her sweetness before kissing a wet trail down her neck.

"I intend to do just that, baby. I love your sweet pussy hugging my cock."

He pressed forward, his dick sliding in easily. She was wet and eager to be filled. He thrust in and slowly pulled out, again and again. Becca's eyes were closed and her lips parted, panting and moaning. He felt Mark's hand on his ass and thrust into her hot cunt while Mark's lubed fingers pushed into his ass. He couldn't hold back his groan of pleasure as Mark grazed his prostate. Becca's eyes flew open and darkened with passion.

"How does it feel?"

Travis groaned. "It feels so good. Mark knows just how to touch and fuck me."

Travis widened his legs as Mark lined his cock up to his back hole. He pushed forward relentlessly, sending pleasure suffusing his veins. Nothing had felt this good before. His cock was buried in his woman, and his man was buried in his ass.

"Aw fuck, baby. This feels amazing. I'm balls deep in Becca and you're balls deep in me. Don't go easy on me. Give it to me hard."

Mark nipped at his earlobe. "I will. Now give it the same to our girl."

Becca was moving restlessly underneath him.

"Oh God, I actually felt your cock swell inside me when he nailed you."

He felt Mark's chuckle on the back of his neck. "Trav likes to get nailed."

Becca pulled up her knees and gripped his biceps.

"So do I."

Travis needed no second urging. He began fucking Becca hard, his cock a pile driver in her cunt. Mark was giving him a pounding in his own ass. The double sensations crashed over him, taking him higher than he had ever been.

"I can't hold back, Becca. Come with me."

Travis reached between them and rubbed circles on her clit. She flew apart in his arms, screaming his name, her cunt clamping down on his cock. He couldn't hold back any longer. He thrust one last time inside her just as Mark thrust once more inside him. He poured his cum into the condom as Mark poured his cum into his ass. His climax ripped through him, holding his body frozen for long moments before he slumped, sated and replete. Mark rolled off him, pulling from Travis's sore ass.

Travis pushed himself up and rolled off of Becca. He didn't want to flatten her like a pancake. He was a big man. He pushed her hair away from her eyes.

"You okay, baby?"

Becca's eyes fluttered open, and she smiled.

"Fuck yeah, I'm okay. That was so hot, watching Mark fuck you while you fucked me. I think I just upped my status in the bad-girl club from minion to upper management."

Travis couldn't hold back his laughter. This woman was a gift.

"Glad we could help. Now maybe we should get some sleep. I'm fucking exhausted. Snuggle with Mark while I take care of the condom."

When Travis returned, the two people he loved most in the world were snoring. Travis shook his head and pulled the covers over himself and Becca. His bad girl looked pretty innocent when she was asleep. He lightly kissed her and cuddled up to her back. This was the first night of many for the three of them.

Chapter 10

Becca approached Addie's door, pulling the cooler of food behind her. The sound of an angry voice halted her. She strained to hear and realized the creepy Randall was visiting again. And apparently, being none too friendly. She pushed open the door with more noise than usual.

"Addie! It's Becca. I hope you're hungry."

Randall's face was red and contorted. He didn't look very handsome at the moment. Addie, on the other hand, looked pale and faint. Becca rushed forward, giving Randall an angry scowl and pulling out her phone. She needed to call Mark. Addie didn't look well.

"What have you done to her? You can't badger an elderly woman, for God's sake. Get out!"

Addie was obviously shaken from her exchange with her nephew, and Becca felt a knot of anger build in her stomach. Mark picked up on the other end as she patted Addie's hand.

"Mark? It's Becca. I'm at Addie Malone's house delivering lunch, and she doesn't look well. Can you come check on her? Please, Mark."

He must have heard something in her voice. He didn't ask any questions except the address. She turned on Randall.

"You didn't answer me."

Randall's eyes narrowed and his lip curled.

"I don't have to answer a little chit like you. I was talking to my aunt. You're the one interfering."

"Sounded more like you were yelling at her. You need to leave. Now."

Randall invaded her personal space.

Bring it on, asshole.

"I'm not done here. I need to talk to my aunt. You need to go."

"Randall, I want you to leave."

They both turned at the sound of Addie's voice. She was breathless, but her words came out firmly.

"Auntie, we need to talk ab—"

Addie shook her head.

"We are done here. You need to go."

"You heard her. Hit the road."

Randall looked at her with contempt.

"This isn't over. I'll be back another day."

"Thanks for the warning. Get out."

Becca pointed to the door, and it opened. Mark had arrived in record time.

"How did you get here so fast?"

"I was in the car coming back from the grocery store, just a few blocks from here."

Mark glanced at Becca and seemed to size up the situation quickly. He knelt next to Addie and opened his medical bag.

"Let's take a look at you, Mrs. Malone. I'm going to listen to your heart." Mark spoke softly, glancing up at Becca and then Randall. Becca pointed to the door again.

"Randall was just leaving."

Randall gave her a look full of pure hate before stomping to the door. She was right behind him to ensure he didn't change his mind. When he crossed the threshold, he grabbed her arm, squeezing so hard she had to steel herself not to wince.

"No one is going to keep me from my aunt. Especially not a nosy girl like you. Mind your own damn business."

Becca almost laughed at his pompous tone. His words reminded her of her favorite cartoon.

And I would have gotten away with it, too, except for you meddling kids!

He finally released her arm and sped away in his car. She rubbed where he had grabbed her as she headed back into the house. Randall was someone who couldn't be trusted, obviously. Mark was taking Addie's blood pressure when she returned. She stayed silent while he examined her and talked to her. Addie's color had returned and she seemed much less agitated.

"Well, Mrs. Malone, your blood pressure is a little high, but you seem okay. Just shook up. Do you want to share what happened here?"

Addie's lips pressed together. "My nephew is an asshole."

The corners of Mark's mouth quirked up.

"I won't argue that point. He's your family, so you would know best."

"Most of the time Randall is charming. Flighty, but charming. He's been visiting me quite a bit lately, so I thought perhaps these were his good days. But lately, he's been badgering me about investing in some real estate deal he's working on. I don't have any interest in investing in real estate at my age. Today he lost his temper and threatened to have me declared incompetent to manage my affairs."

Becca gasped. "That's terrible. But it would never work, Addie. You have the most sound mind of anyone I know."

Addie harrumphed in disgust. "Of course I do. But that doesn't mean Randall won't make trouble."

Mark put away his stethoscope and blood-pressure cuff. "I can talk to Travis if you like. He can do some research on this subject."

Addie gave Mark a relieved look. "I would appreciate that. I don't want to have to convince a judge that I can make my own decisions."

Mark patted her hand. "I agree with Becca. You seem of very sound mind to me."

Addie leaned back on the sofa and sighed. "I'm wore out after his visit. Becca, dear, will you bring my tray out here? I think I'll eat here in front of the television."

"Of course, Addie."

Mark helped Becca settle Addie in the living room with a TV tray and her lunch. Becca pulled Mark into the kitchen.

"Randall the rat cannot be trusted."

Mark chuckled. "You've given him a nickname? He seemed slimy to me. I've seen his type in Chicago. All talk. No substance."

"He gives me the heebie-jeebies. He leered at me last time, all charm. This time he was a jerk. I don't trust him at all."

Mark sighed and leaned against the kitchen counter. "Honestly, neither do I. I got a weird feeling when I met him. I'll call Travis. Maybe he can check up on this guy and the laws surrounding declaring someone incompetent in the state of Florida. Good thing he didn't wait to pass his bar exam here. He's not going to have much downtime."

Becca stood on her tiptoes and kissed Mark lightly. He tasted like wintergreen Life Savers.

"Thank you for coming. And so quickly, too. I couldn't believe when you opened the door. Do you always have your medical bag with you?"

Mark nodded. "Hell, yes. You never know when you are going to need it. I've tended to accident victims and next-door neighbors. I delivered a baby at a Bulls game once."

Becca giggled. "Did they name him Michael Jordan?"

Mark laughed, grabbed his medical bag, and headed to the door. "The husband wanted to, but the wife overruled him. They named him Mark, after the doctor who delivered him."

Becca trailed after him. "Aw, that's sweet."

"That's me. Dr. Awfully Sweet. Now, are we all going to Charlie's reopening tomorrow night?"

"I wouldn't miss it."

Mark leaned in and stole a quick kiss that left her breathless and her lips tingling.

"Great. We'll pick you up at six, okay? And stay away from Randall the rat. He looked none too happy with you when he left. I don't want him taking his anger out on you."

Becca arched a sculpted eyebrow. "I'm not afraid of him. I can take him. Easy. He's obviously out of shape."

Mark gave her a stern look. "Let's not test that theory. Stay away from him, princess. Don't make me spank you."

Becca laughed. "Let's not test the theory that a spanking is an actual punishment for me."

Mark shook his head as he headed to his car. "I think we already know the answer. I'll have to be more creative."

Becca's pussy tingled in anticipation. She was learning to love their creativity.

* * * *

Mark shuffled the deck of cards and began to deal the hand.

"Five-card stud. Deuces wild."

The men anted, and Mark looked at his cards. They sucked. He tossed them down.

"I'm out."

Jack grimaced. "Me, too."

Zach glanced around the table and then threw in another poker chip. "I'm in."

Chase grinned and followed suit. "Me, too."

Ryan eyed Zach before tossing in his chip. "I'm in, too."

Travis tapped his cards on the table and called, "I'm in."

"Ryan, have you talked to Becca today?"

Ryan shook his head and tossed away three cards. Mark dealt him three more.

"Nope, not since our fun-filled conversation at firehouse bingo."

"I saw her earlier. She was delivering lunch to Addie Malone."

Jack smiled. "Our sister sure does a lot for the community. And she loves Addie. Nice woman."

"Well, her nephew isn't a nice man. He was there threatening Addie and being a general prick to Becca."

He had Ryan's full attention.

"He did something to Becca? What was he threatening, and why didn't someone call me?"

"He didn't do anything illegal. He wants Addie to invest in some real estate deal. She doesn't want to, and he threatened to have her declared incompetent. Which is where Travis comes into this."

Travis looked up from his cards. "Me? How do I come into this? I wasn't even there."

Mark continued dealing. "I told Addie you would check out how difficult it is in the state of Florida to have someone declared incompetent. I also thought you might check out this Randall guy and see if you can find out anything about him."

Travis grimaced. "I don't have too many contacts in this state yet, but maybe Mike does. He's been a lawyer in this town for forty years, he's bound to have some connections. And I will research that. Is she incompetent? Does she need help?"

Mark barked with laughter. "She's the most lucid woman you could want to meet."

Chase nodded. "Addie would be classified as one woman who can take care of herself. She's a force to be reckoned with. Shit, I'm out."

It was down to Travis, Zach, and Ryan. Ryan gave Zach a narrow-eyed look.

"I think you're full of shit, Zach. I call. Let's see what you got. I got a pair of aces."

Zach smiled and laid his cards down. "Three of a kind."

"You asshole. I oughta—"

"Full house." Travis laid his cards on the table.

Zach started laughing. "Looks like we have a new card shark to watch out for. He's gonna clean us all out tonight."

Ryan just laughed as Travis swept up all the chips.

"Do I need to make a visit to this Randall guy? Let him know that law enforcement is interested in his activities?"

Mark shrugged. "Couldn't hurt. He was telling Becca to stop interfering. He looked at her like he hated her. Frankly, I was glad I was there."

"Dammit, Becca should have called me."

Jack shook his head and took the deck of cards from Mark.

"Uh-uh, big brother. What did Becca ream our asses about at bingo? Thinking she can't take care of herself. This falls into that category. You go all big-brother sheriff on her, she's going to lose it."

"This isn't about getting her heart broke, this is about something completely different. Her safety. I'm the law in this town, and I don't like trouble in Plenty."

Zach leaned back in his chair. "No one wants trouble in Plenty. If you're going to interfere, keep a low profile and don't let her know about it."

Ryan took a drink from his longneck. "I invented low profile."

* * * *

She was being watched. She could feel eyes following her as she quickly did her errands. She stopped in the hardware store on Main to pick up new lightbulbs for the shop then headed to the diner to pick up lunch. She stepped into the restaurant, waited a minute, then stepped out, running right into the wall that was Deputy Jason, knocking the breath right out of her.

"Whoa! Are you okay, Becca?"

Becca stepped back to catch her breath. Deputy Jason Aldridge was a mountain of a man, every inch muscle.

"Yeah, I think so. What the hell are you doing following me? And don't say you're not, Jason. I can tell when you're lying. I've been able to tell since high school when you dumped me to take Tammy Beaterman to the homecoming dance."

"Aw shit, Becca. Are you ever going to let me live that down? I've said I'm sorry about a hundred times. You were a nice girl, and every guy in school knew Tammy put out."

And still did if the gossip was true.

"I ought to stomp on your foot for calling me a nice girl. But I suppose karma may have taken care of things for me. I heard some boys got more than they bargained for after spending time in the backseat with Tammy. They ended up at the free clinic in Tampa getting some antibiotics."

A dark red stained Jason's cheeks.

"Unlike some dumbasses, I always suited up with Tammy. Man's got to take care of himself. Now, how did you know I was following you?"

Becca rolled her eyes. "I could feel someone following me. So why are you following me?"

Jason hooked his thumbs in his gun belt. "I shouldn't tell you this, but your brother asked me to keep an eye on you. Said some guy isn't too happy with you. We also have a patrol driving by Addie Malone's house every hour."

Becca felt her face get warm with anger and frustration. *My overprotective brothers strike again.* She was glad they were watching over Addie, but she could take care of herself.

"Well, your services are no longer needed. You can go write parking tickets or do whatever it is that Ryan's deputies do on a small-town Tuesday afternoon. I'm in between clients this afternoon and have things I need to get done."

Jason shook his head. "No can do. The boss says to keep an eye on you, that's what I gotta do."

Becca grabbed the deputy's arm and tugged him into the diner. "Well, if you're going to hang around you can buy me lunch and then tell me why my brother is having me followed."

* * * *

Mark pushed open the door of Becca's hair salon, the Snip and Sing, his gaze immediately finding his beautiful woman giving one of the town deputies a haircut. The shop was empty for a Tuesday afternoon.

She looked pretty in white capris with a pink T-shirt and pink Converse tennis shoes. Her long hair was clipped back from her face with a sparkly barrette. She was so gorgeous, Mark had to restrain himself from bending her over the back of a chair and showing her how he really felt. He settled for a soft kiss on her full, cherry-red lips.

"Hey, sweetheart. Any chance of getting a haircut today? I have a break in between patients."

Becca waved him over to a chair. "Sure. Let me just finish with Deputy Jason here. Mark, have you met Jason Aldridge?"

Mark shook his head and extended his hand to the handsome deputy. He felt a little twinge of jealousy at how Becca smiled at the man.

"No, I haven't. Nice to meet you, Deputy. I'm Mark Miller."

Jason's grip was firm. "Nice to meet you, too. I believe your sister is going to marry my boss, Ryan."

Mark laughed. "That's the way I hear it. God help him."

"She seems like a nice girl. Just like Becca."

Mark was surprised when Becca gave the deputy's hair a tug. "Hey, what did I say about calling me a nice girl? I swear, men never learn. Speaking of never learning, Mark, do you know why Deputy Jason is here today?"

Mark relaxed in a chair and picked up a magazine.

"For a haircut?"

Becca's lips twisted into a strange smile.

"That was just a nice bonus for him. It seems my big brother is concerned for my safety and assigned him to watch over me. Somehow, he learned about my exchange with Addie's nephew. I wonder how he found out about that?"

Mark set the magazine down. The silence stretched on for a while. He was so screwed.

"About that, well, I mentioned it at poker last night."

"Uh-huh, did you tell him to watch over me?"

Becca's voice was deceptively soft. She was pissed.

Mark jumped to his feet. "No, I did not. He mentioned that he would keep an eye out, and I said I thought it was a good idea. I didn't know he would go to this extreme. I swear. I would have told him that Travis and I could watch over you just fine."

From the look on her face, she wasn't any happier.

"I don't need a bunch of overprotective alpha males watching over me. I am capable of taking care of myself. I know Randall's type, and they are nothing but cowards. I could kick his ass with one hand tied behind my back. I had to grow up tough with two brothers like Ryan and Jack."

"I'm not an overprotective alpha male," the deputy protested.

Becca rolled her eyes. "The hell you aren't. The poor woman who ends up with you will need a backbone of steel or you'll boss her around terribly. And your haircut is done, and so is your shift. Go tell Ryan if he wants to assign a babysitter he can damn well do it himself."

The deputy hopped out of the chair and headed for the door.

"Ryan is going to be upset that you've sent me back to the station."

"He'll get over it. If he has a problem, tell him to talk to me instead of going behind my back."

The deputy looked nervous about delivering the message but shoved his hat on his head and nodded.

"Okay. You really are one tough cookie, Becca. I think I should have kept our date to the homecoming dance."

Becca smirked. "You lost your chance with me in high school."

Mark put his arm around her shoulders and pulled her close. "She's already spoken for, Deputy."

Deputy Jason grinned and headed out the door with a wave. Becca's shoulders were stiff under his arm.

"Becca, I'm sorry."

She turned toward him, worrying her bottom lip with her teeth.

"Please don't bring Ryan into things anymore, okay? He overreacts. Assigning a deputy to me full-time is an overreaction, don't you agree?"

"Yes, I do agree. I didn't know he would do anything like this. I just kind of thought we would all keep alert for any moves Randall might make."

Becca fell back into a chair and sighed. "Well, now you know what I've been living with. I'd like to keep our business our business."

Mark leaned down and brushed her lips with his. He could smell the soft floral fragrance of her shampoo and feel the warmth of her skin.

"Agreed. Do you want me to talk to Ryan?"

Becca gave him an evil smile.

"Oh no, handsome. I'll handle my brother."

Chapter 11

The aroma of tomato sauce and Italian herbs filled the air at Charlie's grand reopening. The restaurant, newly renovated after the arson at Christmastime, was larger and more comfortable than ever. Charlie's husbands had managed to negotiate taking over the real estate office next door. The pizza parlor was now twice its original size and still packed to the gills with customers.

Becca admired the brand-new booths, tables, and chairs, all done in honey oak with dark-red cushions. The walls were covered with black-and-white photos of the town from years past. The open kitchen took up one complete side of the restaurant, and they had added barstools to the counters so that single patrons could eat and watch the food being prepared. Zach and Chase Harper had been the contractors, and they had outdone themselves on this job. They were all celebrating the reopening of their favorite pizza parlor. The only pizza parlor in Plenty, for that matter.

Chase lifted his longneck. "To the new Charlie's and the end of a great job. I can't wait to eat Charlie's pizza tonight."

Zach, Cassie, Ryan, Jack, Jillian, Travis, Mark, and Becca all lifted their glasses to toast the new restaurant. Becca sipped at her red wine. She had yet to discuss her favorite deputy with Ryan. Ryan had been strangely quiet tonight, studiously avoiding talking to her. She hated to break the jovial vibe, but she had a few things to say.

"I spent some quality time with Deputy Jason yesterday. I haven't spent that much time with him since I dated him in high school."

Jillian frowned and glanced at her brother and Travis.

"Why were you spending time with Jason? He's a nice guy. We should fix him up with someone."

Zach shook his head. "Probably not a good idea. When Jason dates these days, he doesn't date to find, if you know what I mean. He just dates to have some fun. He hasn't been the same since Gabe left."

Travis took a pull on his beer bottle. "Were they in love?"

Zach looked shocked, and Chase, Ryan, and Jack started laughing. Jack held up a hand with a grin.

"Fuck, no. Jason and Gabe are best friends and cousins. They shared women together, and everyone thought they would settle down with one woman. Gabe and Jason both enlisted together, but Jason got out and became a deputy. Apparently, Gabe has never been the same since he left Afghanistan. He hasn't come back to Plenty, and I'm not sure anyone knows where he is."

Zach had a tense look on his face. He had been a Navy SEAL, and Becca was sure he had seen some of the same horrors that now haunted Gabe.

"A man changes in war. It's how he survives."

No one argued Zach's simple and to-the-point statement. Cassie slid her hand over Zach's and squeezed, giving him a smile full of love. For a moment, they were the only two people in the room in each other's eyes.

Jillian smiled indulgently. "So why were you spending so much time with Jason?"

Becca leaned back in her chair. "You should ask Ryan."

Jillian turned to Ryan. "Okay, Ryan, you tell us."

Ryan looked distinctly discomfited. "I asked Jason to keep an eye on Becca."

Jillian looked around the quiet table. No one spoke. "Um, why?"

"Were you aware that Addie's nephew Randall threatened her?"

Jillian shrugged her shoulders. "Sure, Becca told us about it on Monday night at the diner. I'd hardly call it threatening. He told her to butt out."

"He told her to butt out or she'd be sorry."

"So? Someone flipped me the bird on the road to Zach and Chase's house the other day. Do you think they intend to hunt me down and actually fuck me if I get in their way again?"

Ryan's face was turning a lovely shade of red. No one could yank his chain like his beloved fiancée.

"They better fucking not. You didn't tell me this."

Jillian chuckled. "Of course not. Do you know how many people have given me the finger in my lifetime? Shit, in Chicago it's a sport. Not one of them has come after me."

Jack shook his head. "You have no sense of self-preservation, baby. Ryan's never going to let you drive again."

"Hah! Let him try to stop me."

Ryan scraped his hand down his face. Becca had to hide her smile. He had his hands full with Jillian.

"I'll deal with you later. Anyway, I was just being cautious. You sent him packing with his tail between his legs and a new haircut, so it was a complete failure."

Becca laid her hand on top of his. "It wasn't a failure. It was completely unneeded. Believe me, if I feel threatened, you'll be the first to know. Okay?"

"Okay. I'm going to have to trust you, I guess."

Becca sighed. "Yes, you are. And high time you did, big brother. Nothing is going to happen to me except a tummy ache from eating too much of Charlie's delicious pizza."

Travis smiled. "I'll join you there. Why don't we drink to leading a boring, small-town life?"

They all raised their glasses in agreement.

* * * *

"This sucks."

Becca tossed her purse on the table in the foyer of Mark and Travis's house.

"Get used to it, babe. That's how life is with a doctor in the family. He gets calls at all hours of the day and night."

Some teenagers had wrecked their pickup truck near the quarries. Mark would be performing surgery as he was the closest certified orthopedic surgeon. Despite changing careers, he had decided to pass the state boards to keep his skills sharp. He had put in too many years not to continue helping when he was needed. As disgruntled as she was, she hoped the kids would all be okay.

"I guess so. You must be used to it after so many years."

Travis shrugged. "I try not to give him a hard time about it. You and I will be curled up in a warm bed, and he'll be on his feet for the next eight hours or so working. I think we got the better end of the deal."

Becca pressed her body close to Travis's.

"We certainly did. This time you won't go to bed alone."

Travis's eyes flared with passion. "No, I won't, will I? I'm really starting to like this."

Becca giggled as her hands wandered down his flat abs to cup his hard cock through his jeans.

"Just starting to like this, huh? Sounds like I need to convince you thoroughly."

Travis arched his hips into her hand. "I have a few ideas of how you can. Are you open-minded?"

"I'm a woman in a relationship with two men who are already in a relationship. I'm the epitome of open-minded."

Travis chuckled. "True. Well, let's get you naked and in the bedroom, shall we? I have a few things I'd like to explore with you...since you're so open-minded."

Becca liked the idea of getting naked and open-minded. She knew the way to the bedroom and left a trail of clothes on her way. She was standing naked when Travis caught up with her, a pile of her discarded clothing in his hands.

"Becca, you're going to have to work harder at getting over your shyness and modesty."

Becca laughed at his mocking tone. She wasn't the least bit shy as she stood before his lustful gaze. She only wanted him naked, too.

"Seems like I'm the only one naked here. I want to see your body, too."

Travis chuckled as he lifted her chin with gentle fingers.

"I'm glad you like what you see. But I have some plans for you first. Are you sure you're okay exploring with me?"

Becca frowned. "Stop treating me like a good little girl. When I'm with you, I feel like anything but."

Travis grinned as he headed for the closet, pulling out a leather duffel bag.

"I don't feel like a good boy with you, either. Is there anything in this bag you'd like to try?"

Travis set the bag on the bed and stood back with his arms crossed over his muscular chest. Curiosity had always been her downfall, and it got the better of her now. She unzipped the bag and rummaged to see what was inside.

Toys.

The bag was filled with all sorts of sex toys. She'd hit the mother lode.

"Gosh, I don't know, Travis. How many can I choose?"

"I should have known you'd enjoy this. Pick what you want, babe. They were chosen with you in mind."

Becca perused the contents of the bag, her arousal hitching higher with each find. She had combed through butt plugs, padded handcuffs, vibrators, silk rope, a blindfold, nipple clamps, and colorful tubes of lubricant before she found what she was looking for. She quickly pulled the blindfold and silk rope out and set them on the bed.

"Is that what you want?"

Travis's eyes had darkened to almost black. His arousal radiated off him so hotly she could feel it.

"One more thing."

She pulled the flogger from the bag and laid it out on the bed. The strands were fur and were soft and silky to the touch.

Travis's gaze never flinched from hers. She knew she had chosen well by his almost-feral expression.

"I get to choose something, too. It's only fair."

Becca stepped back from the bag so he could choose. The deliciousness of not knowing what he would choose sent cream gushing from her pussy. Anything he chose would be pleasurable. They wouldn't be getting bored in bed anytime soon with such bounty.

He pulled out a red tube of lubricant and then tossed a butt plug on the bed before returning the bag to the closet. Her ass clenched as she imagined it pressed into her back hole. She'd never had anything there but found the vision darkly erotic.

He leaned down and captured her lips with his own. She could feel the scruff on his cheek and smell his masculine scent. It overwhelmed her senses, and she slowly released her hold on reality and let herself surrender to the pleasure. Her senses heightened and the room faded away until there was only her and Travis. His lips, his hands, became her whole world.

His fingers were like flames licking her skin. She moaned as his mouth traveled across her jaw and down the sensitive cord of her neck. She arched against him to give him better access and press her overheated flesh against his hard body. His hard cock was pressed into her soft belly, telling her he wanted her the same way. She trailed her fingers across the denim stretched tight over his straining dick. She dropped to her knees, tugging at his zipper. She needed to taste him. His hands caught her and pulled her back up.

"Whoa, babe. I want your sweet mouth on me, but not yet. I have plans first."

Becca stuck out her lower lip.

"But I want your cock in my mouth."

Travis grinned and tugged her toward the bed.

"I want that, too. Soon."

He pressed her back onto the pillows, the sheets cool under her heated skin. He dragged the silk rope across her belly, sending a shiver up her spine. She was pouring honey from her pussy as she envisioned what he had in store for her. He ran his hands down her arms and encircled her wrists with the slippery rope before pulling her hands over her head and anchoring them to the headboard.

"Tug."

She pulled, but the rope held fast. Her nipples peaked and her pussy clenched as he moved down to the end of the bed, repeating the process with each ankle. She was spread wide and helpless and already on the edge of climax. He ran a finger through her drenched pussy.

"Very wet. Do you want to be fucked, Becca?"

She licked her suddenly dry lips. She couldn't lie.

"More than anything."

"Well, you're going to have to wait. I want to play a little more."

Travis picked up the black blindfold and dangled it in front of her face.

"Close your eyes, sweetness."

He wrapped the soft fabric around her eyes, robing her in darkness. Her other senses sharpened. She could feel the brush of the hair on his arms and felt his breath against her skin. His tongue traced a wet path down in the valley between her breasts and dipped into her belly button, drawing a giggle from her. His fingers tickled her ribs before plucking at her already painfully hard nipples. She arched her back in an effort to urge his mouth to them. He chuckled.

"All in good time, my sweet. First, another toy."

She felt the cold of the lube as it trickled down her crack and then Travis's fingers circling her back hole. He pressed with his finger and her muscles gave way.

"Breathe, Becca. Don't hold your breath. I hope you like this."

More lube and another finger pressed inside, stretching her ass. It didn't hurt or burn as she expected. She just felt some pressure and then she felt full. She couldn't imagine what it would be like to have a cock up there.

"I don't think your cock will fit in there."

Travis chuckled.

"Not tonight it won't. I'm going to put a plug in there tonight to start gently stretching you. In a few weeks, our cocks will fit just fine. Just relax for me."

She blew out a breath just as the plug started pressing against her tight hole. This time when her muscles gave way, she felt the burn but no real pain. It was only when Travis began moving the plug in and out she felt electricity run through her body. She tried to move with it, but the restraints held her still.

She felt Travis's breath on her nipples and then his mouth. He licked, sucked, and nipped at each nipple until they stood proud and erect. The pads of his fingers caressed his handiwork before she felt the bed move and he was gone for a moment. She heard water in the bathroom, and then he was next to her again. She could feel the heat from his body as he leaned over her.

"I want you to try something tonight. This is the red tube. Just go with it."

She felt something cold and wet drip on each nipple. She shivered and waited for something to happen.

"Trav, what is this? Oh!"

The cold had transformed into a simmering heat. Each moment that passed raised the temperature on her nipples until they felt as if hot wax had been dripped on them. She moaned as arrows of pleasure and pain shot to her pussy and clit. She tugged at her restraints as she tried to twist away from the unrelenting heat.

The first lick on her swollen clit took her breath away. The second and third sent her floating above the bed on a cloud of pleasure. The heat on her nipples radiated through her body and was getting all mixed up in the pleasure his talented tongue brought her. She was teetering on the edge of orgasm when he sucked her clit into his mouth, scraping his teeth lightly across the sensitive flesh.

She screamed his name over and over as her body shook. She pulled and tugged at her restraints, but they held fast as she rode the pleasure all the way to the end. She closed her eyes as she lay limp and breathing hard. His hands skimmed over her extrasensitive flesh, starting her climb toward orgasm again.

"For the love of God, Travis, have some mercy."

"No mercy tonight, baby. You're open-minded, remember?"

She barely had time to register his words when she felt the brush of fur against her sensitized skin. Travis was using the fur flogger to drive her insane. Each brush of the soft fur sent tingles through her body and straight to her clit. He tickled her nipples, gliding the fur round and round each tip until it was painfully hard. She couldn't hold back her moan.

"Travis!"

She felt a soothing hand on her belly.

"I know, baby. Relax into it."

This time the soft brushes became soft whips. He gently whipped her thighs with the fur strands. There was no pain, only pleasure. It almost felt like being massaged by the most luxurious fur. Travis moved the flogger up her belly and to her straining breasts. She arched her body into the soft whips, begging him to go harder and faster. He ignored her, setting up his own rhythm until she was begging him to do anything, just please, please let her come.

She heard the flogger drop on the floor with a thud and the crinkle of a condom wrapper. Travis was going to fuck her and, if she had anything to say about it, fuck her hard.

* * * *

Travis let his gaze roam over his beautiful Becca. Her skin was flushed a rosy pink from the flogger, her breath was coming in pants, and her thighs were sticky and shiny from her juices. He couldn't wait to bury himself balls deep inside her. He quickly shucked his clothes off and tossed them aside before straddling her on the bed and rolling the condom down his aching cock. He nudged her slit with the blunt tip of his cock and let it slide up and down, rubbing her honey all over the condom. She was so wet he would glide in easily.

"Are you ready for me, sweetness?"

She tugged at her restraints. "I want to touch you, too."

He leaned forward and buried his nose in her neck where it met her shoulder. He breathed in her sweet scent, and his cock hardened painfully. He pressed his cock forward into her heat, groaning as her tight pussy enfolded him. She was so tight and wet. The plug made the fit even more snug than before. She squeezed her muscles and his cock throbbed in response. Nothing felt the way fucking Becca felt. It was a singular experience he wanted the rest of his life.

He thrust slowly at first, trying to hold on to the shred of control he had left. As he picked up speed, he thrust harder until his balls were pulled up close to his body and the pressure in his lower back became unbearable. He reached between them and rubbed circles around her clit. Her pussy clamped down on his cock as her climax swept through her. He followed her over, letting the waves crash through his body. He slumped on top of her as they subsided, leaving him wrung out but exalted. They were amazing together. His natural reticence was shot to hell, leaving him feeling triumphant. They had found their third.

"I know I'm squishing you. I swear I'll move in a minute."

He felt more than heard her giggle. He levered himself up and quickly disposed of the condom before untying her ankles and wrists. He gently massaged them and checked for bruising. He then slowly pulled the plug from her bottom and threw it in the bathroom sink for washing.

She pulled her blindfold off and tossed it aside, giving him a saucy smile.

"It just gets better and better."

Travis stretched out next to her and pulled her close.

"It always will, baby. It always will."

* * * *

Travis was bringing her home the next morning when she saw Ryan's police SUV. She was almost ready to lay into him for spying on her when she realized he wasn't alone. Deputy Jason had his own vehicle there, and they seemed to be investigating something. Travis pulled into her driveway, and they both headed for Ryan to find out what had happened.

"Hey, big brother, what's going on here?"

Ryan had an irritated expression on his face. He hated crime in his town.

"Vandals. Probably kids. They knocked down all the mailboxes in the condo complex."

Becca looked around, and sure enough every mailbox for as far as she could see had been knocked from its post.

"You think everything is kids."

Ryan chuckled. "Why would an adult knock off mailboxes? This is a juvenile crime, baby girl. Shit, I mean Becca."

Becca gave her brother a smile. He really was trying.

"Why would a juvenile knock down mailboxes, then? Seems like a dumb crime all the way around."

Deputy Jason walked up with a grin. "Criminals aren't usually the sharpest tools in the shed. Morning, Becca."

Becca grinned back. "Morning, Jason. Still, it seems like a stupid crime. What do they gain?"

Travis's arm came around her and pulled her close. Possessive. She liked it. It seemed he was a wee jealous of Deputy Jason.

"They don't gain anything but the thrill, babe. That's enough for them. For a while, anyway."

Ryan nodded. "Probably just some high school kids joyriding and drinking some beer, laughing their asses off. It's a pain in the ass, but personally, I'd rather have this sort of mayhem than some of the other options. Drugs, gangs. Hell, you probably saw your share in Chicago, Travis."

"Unfortunately, yes. This seems pretty innocent in comparison."

Jason shrugged. "We'll take everyone's statement anyway and make the report. Did you see or hear anything last night, Becca?"

Becca felt her face get warm. "Um, no."

Ryan shooed Jason away. "Go take their statement over there. Mrs. Dawson said she saw a car peeling out of here last night."

Ryan gave her and Travis a knowing look. He had obviously seen them drive up this morning.

"Is Mark still at the hospital? I worked that accident last night. It's good to have another doctor in town. Especially a surgeon who's available in an emergency."

Travis's body relaxed next to hers. Ryan wasn't going to bring up the obvious.

"He texted me a few minutes ago and said he was wrapping things up. He'll go home and get a few hours of sleep and head into the office for appointments."

"He gets less sleep than I do."

"He's used to it. He loves what he does."

"Well, I'll let you get going. We need to take statements and head out of here. Police cars always draw a crowd."

Becca and Travis headed into her condo. She started bustling in the kitchen making coffee. Travis was watching her closely.

"Are you embarrassed?"

Becca whirled around. "No! No, I'm not embarrassed."

"It would be normal if you were. I don't think my brothers and sisters want to know a whole lot about my sex life."

"Ryan doesn't know anything, but I know more about his sex life than I ever wanted to. Hell, I've heard him, Jack, and Jillian having sex right here in this condo. She's a screamer, for fuck's sake. They were like rutting animals. That's more than anyone should know about their sibling."

Travis laughed. "You're a screamer, too, babe. And I'm not complaining at all."

Chapter 12

"Oh, Cassie, you look amazing!"

Cassie did look amazing. The white satin-and-lace gown clung softly to her small frame, making her look elegant and sophisticated. She was having her wedding-dress fitting, and Jillian and Becca were also getting fitted for their bridesmaid dresses. Becca lifted Cassie's hair high on top of her head and placed the veil on top.

"I think you should wear your hair up. I can do a sort of chignon with some curls here. It will give the veil a lovely place to sit."

Cassie considered her reflection for a moment. "Not down? Zach and Chase love my hair down."

"We can do it down, too. I can iron it straight or do a fall of curls with a half-up, half-down look. Jillian?"

Jillian was fussing with the top of her bridesmaid dress. It was very formfitting and showed off both Jillian's and Becca's assets.

"I like it up. It's a special day. You should have a special style."

Cassie pulled the veil off and sighed. "I'll decide later."

Becca took the veil and carefully placed it in tissue paper.

"Not too much later. We need to have a hair-and-makeup run-through prior to the wedding. Ticktock."

"Can you believe how quickly the time is going? In less than a month, I'll be Mrs. Zach and Chase Harper."

Cassie was glowing with love for her men. Becca was starting to feel some hope she herself might be that happy someday, too.

Jillian fiddled with the long hem of her dress. "And I'll soon be Mrs. Ryan and Jackson Parks. And Becca will be Mrs. Mark and Travis Miller-Andrews."

Becca felt herself blush. "Things haven't gotten that far. We're dating."

Jillian rolled her eyes. "Is that what the kids are calling it these days? Ryan told me he saw you coming home yesterday morning with Travis."

"Well, shit, it was none of his damn business."

Jillian laughed and shrugged off the strapless navy-blue dress with a relieved sigh. Becca knew Jillian preferred jeans and T-shirts.

"Of course it wasn't, which I told him. He said he behaved."

"He did. I'll give him that. I miss having you guys living close to me. You're never there anymore."

Cassie spent most nights at Zach and Chase's house, and Jillian was spending more and more nights with Ryan and Jackson. Jillian helped Cassie with the tiny pearl buttons on the back of the dress.

"Glad I wasn't home. A bunch of drunk teenagers, out for a joyride, knocking at mailboxes? No thanks. I like sleeping through the night."

Cassie frowned. "Funny thing, though. None of the neighbors heard or saw much. One neighbor thought she heard a car leaving, but all in all, the deed was done quietly."

Jillian shrugged. "Okay, so the teenagers didn't make a lot of noise. It was the middle of the night. Everyone was sleeping. You have a suspicious mind."

It was Cassie's turn to roll her eyes. "If you had my past, you would be suspicious, too."

"I'm surprised my brother didn't go into overprotective mode and force us all to move out of the condo complex and into protective custody until these hooligans are brought to justice."

Jillian laughed. "I'm sure it crossed his mind. He's a very protective man, which makes me love him and want to beat him over the head all at the same time."

Becca shook her head. "Better you than me dealing with him. Jack's not much more reasonable."

"They're trying. It's not easy for your brothers to not worry about you. But I vow to try and keep them so busy they don't have time."

Cassie waggled her eyebrows. "How do you plan to do that?"

"The usual way. Naughty lingerie and sex toys."

Becca laughed. "Well, thank you. I think."

Jillian gave a blissful sigh. "It's no hardship. Believe me. You just have to do one thing for me."

"What's that?"

"Take good care of Mark and Travis. They have totally fallen for you. They have a goofy look on their face whenever you're in the room or even just mentioned."

Becca grinned. "I'll take very good care of them."

She was pretty sure she had the very same look.

* * * *

Becca twirled in her new black pumps with a very unsensible three-and-a-half-inch heel. She had paired them with a low-slung skinny black skirt that stopped midthigh and a ruffled white blouse. A black belt made her waist look tiny and her breasts generous. She was beginning to really appreciate her curves. Her men worshipped them every time they were together.

They were taking her to Eighties Night at Party Like a Rock Star, a brand-new bar on the edge of town. Quickly becoming known simply as The Party, it was owned by a former B-grade rock star who had retired and moved to Plenty. He ran The Party as a hobby and diversion, liking the fact that no one in Plenty was impressed by his past.

A rap on the front door had her hurrying to see her men. They had all been busy, and she hadn't been able to spend time with them in a few days. She pulled open the door and Mark stood there with a sexy grin. He looked gorgeous as all hell in well-washed blue jeans and a navy button-down shirt. His blond hair was growing a little longer at her urging. She loved to run her fingers through it, feeling the silky texture.

"Hey, sweetie. You gonna let me in?"

Becca stepped back, peering out the door after Mark entered.

"Where's Travis?"

Mark pulled Becca into his arms and ran his hands down her back, sending shivers down her spine.

"Travis got caught up in some business in Orlando. He'll meet us at the bar. I'll have you to myself for a couple of hours."

Then his lips were on hers and she forgot how empty the last two days had been. His lips caressed hers as his tongue explored her mouth sensuously. By the time he pulled back, she was breathless and wet. She grabbed his arm and started pulling him toward the bedroom. She needed him inside her. Now.

"Whoa, baby. What about The Party?"

"We'll still go. After."

"After, huh? You have a naughty mind. I love it."

Becca peeked at him from under her lashes. "Perhaps you should punish me for having such naughty thoughts."

Mark's grin grew wider and a hell of a lot more evil.

"I wouldn't want to punish you for something I enjoy." He laughed at her crestfallen expression. "Have you been having naughty thoughts for the last two days? Did you touch yourself while you were fantasizing?"

Becca was practically panting with anticipation. She nodded. "I couldn't help it. I can't stop thinking about us. Together."

Mark's hands felt hot as he ran them up her arms, over her shoulders, and over the sensitive skin of the nape of her neck to capture her hair and tangle his fingers in it. He gave it a gentle tug so she was looking deeply into his blue eyes, dark with passion.

"I will punish you for that. Your pleasure belongs to us now, Becca. Travis and I control it. You don't come unless we decide you come. Do you understand?"

She knew she should be arguing with his Neanderthal declaration of male control, but she found herself melting against him, nodding in acquiescence. She wanted them to have control in the bedroom. She wanted to put away all the things she needed to think about every day as a business owner and a civic volunteer and lie back and let them take control.

"Good. For your disobedience, you're going to get a spanking. Then I'm going to fuck you so you know who's in charge in the bedroom."

Becca lowered her eyes demurely. "Yes, Sir."

Mark chuckled. "Sir, huh? I've never been called Sir in the bedroom, but I think I like it."

Mark smacked her bottom hard, and even through her skirt and panties it made her ass cheek warm. Her panties were soaked and her nipples were hard and rubbing against the lace of her bra. She wanted more. Much more.

"You can continue to call me Sir. Into the bedroom. Now."

* * * *

Mark walked behind Becca, her ass swaying provocatively in her tight black skirt. He couldn't wait to spank her pert, round bottom. She was going to come at least twice before they left for the bar. She stopped and rounded on her high heels to face him. She was as turned on as he was, her face flushed and her chest rising and falling rapidly. He knew if he ran a finger through her pussy it would be dripping honey for him. It was clear she loved the idea of being punished.

"Strip for me. Slowly. You can keep the shoes on."

Mark sat on the bed to enjoy the show. Becca slowly plucked at the buttons on her blouse before pushing it off her shoulders. She tossed it casually in his lap with a saucy smile. Her bra was a lacy push-up type, and he could see her tight nipples outlined clearly. She pivoted on her high heels so his view was now her curvy backside.

She reached to her side and slowly lowered the zipper of her skirt tooth by tooth. Mark's cock was rock hard and pressing against his own button fly. He almost groaned as she bent at the waist to slide the skirt down her shapely legs, revealing the teeny black thong underneath. The string split the round globes of her ass, sending his mind thinking about what it would be like to be buried deep inside that ass.

She stepped out of it, turned back to him, and tossed it at him. He caught it easily and added it to the growing pile of clothes next to him. His only regret was that he wasn't having Becca strip to music. Now that would really be something.

Becca paused for a moment. Her pink tongue snaked out to wet her full lips. Mark vowed those same lips would be wrapped around his cock tonight. His dick was demanding action immediately, but Mark tamped down his own arousal. It was too delicious watching Becca strip for his pleasure.

She reached behind her, and with a flick of her fingers the lacy bra went slack. She pulled it down her arms and tossed it at his head. He caught it out of the air a split second before he was pelted in the face with her lingerie. With a grin, he twirled it in his hands, salivating at the sight of her breasts bared for his gaze. She cupped them, lifting them as if in offering. He would definitely be taking her up on her offer. Soon.

She trailed her hands lightly down her torso to hook her fingers in the sides of the thong. She ran her hands teasingly around the edge, just pulling them down a few inches before pulling them up again.

"Looks like someone wants her spanking to be harder and longer. Teasing me will make your punishment worse."

Becca didn't bat an eyelash. She giggled and played with the elastic a little more, making his cock jump in his pants. His little rebel was so spanked. She finally, ever so slowly, slid the black thong down her legs before tossing it in the air. He caught it and brought it to his nose. The thong was soaked, and he could easily smell the sweet musk of her arousal. He could bend her over the edge of the bed right now and thrust himself to the hilt.

Not yet.

She stood before him, every inch of her creamy skin bared for his inspection. He took his time taking her sexy body in from the tips of her candy-apple-red toenails to the top of her golden-blonde hair. She was gorgeous, and he felt a possessive tug in his chest. She belonged to them.

He pointed to the floor in front of where he lounged on the bed. She got the hint immediately, and she eagerly hit her knees, licking her lips. She was definitely going to get a big, hard cock in her mouth. He popped open his fly and pulled out his aching dick, stroking it up and down with a tortured groan. Her blue eyes were dark with desire. It would be his pleasure and Travis's to fulfill those desires for the next fifty years or so.

"Suck me, baby. Show me what a bad girl can do with her mouth."

"Yes, Sir."

Becca's voice was husky and breathless. She leaned forward, grasping his cock at the base, and licked around the reddish-purple mushroom head. Mark had to bite back his moan of pleasure as her tongue flicked his cock from balls to tip before engulfing as much as she could swallow in her wet, hot mouth. He leaned back on his elbow while his other hand tangled in her long hair. It slipped through his fingers like silk. He knew her pussy would feel just as silky when he thrust every inch he had to give her in its warmth.

"That's it, sweetness. Suck and lick me. You know you love my cock in your mouth, don't you?"

She nodded wordlessly as her head bobbed up and down on his swollen shaft. Her talented fingers rolled his balls, and he couldn't stop the groan torn from his throat. He wouldn't last long at this rate. He was almost over the edge. His breathing was ragged when she lightly scraped her teeth along the sensitive skin of his shaft. It was all he needed to send him over.

He shoved his cock deep into her throat and held it there as his climax ripped through him. Her throat worked to keep up with the cum he shot deep into her mouth, the waves sending shudders of pleasure through him. He finally fell back on the bed, spent and drained. Becca licked him clean before climbing on the bed next to him and cuddling close. Her fingers trailed up and down his chest and abdomen, and despite coming hard just moments before, he felt his cock begin to stir. How did he and Travis get so lucky?

* * * *

Becca absorbed Mark's warmth as she cuddled close to him. She could smell the tang from his aftershave and the masculine smell that was all his. She trailed kisses down the strong column of his neck and tried to pull his shirt over his head. She wanted him naked and fucking her.

"Not yet, baby. You still have to be punished."

Becca pouted. "I'm not sure it's really fair. No one told me I wasn't allowed to touch myself."

Mark sat up with a laugh, patting his lap. "You don't want fair. You want to be spanked. Am I wrong?"

Becca wasn't a liar. She sighed in surrender. "No, you're not wrong."

Mark patted his lap again. "Then drape yourself across my knees and take your punishment like a big girl. You're going to love my spankings."

Becca was pretty sure she was going to love it, too, since she had enjoyed Travis spanking her. She was practically wriggling with excitement as she lay on his lap, her head hanging down and her ass in the air. His warm hand rubbed circles on her ass cheeks, sending tingles straight to her pussy and clit. She knew she was dripping cream in anticipation.

"Ready, baby?"

She never had a chance to answer before his hand came down on her ass. It stung for a moment, and then the heat started spreading from her bottom to her cunt. She had barely caught her breath before his hand came down again and again. He rained blows on her ass, sending her arousal into outer space and making her bite her lip to keep from begging to come. He paused and trailed his fingertips across her hot cheeks.

"Are you still with me, Becca? Do you want me to stop?"

Her ass was on fire and her honey had dripped down her thighs. She bent further and stuck her ass high in the air.

"No, don't stop."

Her voice sounded strained, but she was sure of what she wanted. She needed more. His hand came down again on her already-sore ass cheeks. The smacks were spread evenly across her bottom and the top of her thighs. Desperate to come, Becca rubbed her clit against his hard thigh, trying to send herself over. He lifted his thigh to give her more direct contact as the spanking continued but lighter and slower now. One more grind against his leg and she exploded. White light blinded her and pleasure crashed through her body until she hung limp and spent over his lap. He petted and soothed her as she came down to earth. He lifted her carefully and laid her on the bed, holding her close, crooning praise in her ear. She had never felt anything like the orgasm she had just experienced.

She trailed her hands down his muscled back.

"You have too many clothes on."

She felt Mark's chuckle. "I guess I need to get naked, huh? Are you okay, sweetness? Did you like your spanking?"

She levered herself up and stared into his sky-blue eyes. "I fucking loved it. I've never come that hard in my life. It was amazing. Promise me you'll do it again."

Mark grinned and pulled his shirt over his head, tossing it aside. "I promise. Travis'll spank you as often as you like, too. We want to keep our woman happy."

"I like the sound of that. Your woman."

Mark stood to pull off his pants and boxer shorts. "Fuck yeah, you're our woman. You're not getting away from us now."

Becca pulled his naked body down on top of hers. "I don't want to get away from you. I'm pretty happy being your woman."

Mark pulled away for a moment to snag a condom from his pants pocket. She grabbed it from his fingers and tore the packet open with her teeth.

"Let me do the honors."

Mark stood very still as she slowly rolled the condom on his hard cock. She caressed his balls before pulling him down again.

"Fuck me. Hard. Sir. Fuck the foreplay."

Mark laughed at her belated use of his title.

"My woman wants to be fucked hard, then she gets fucked hard. Spread your legs, sweetie."

Becca spread her thighs, and Mark caught them and wrapped them around his waist. The blunt edge of his cock pressed against her cunt, and he entered her slowly inch by inch, stretching her with his girth. She moaned as he thrust to the hilt. She loved feeling so full.

"Ready to ride, baby?"

"Yes, Mark, give it to me."

Mark pulled out almost all the way before slamming back into her creaming pussy. She lifted and met his thrust, grinding her already swollen and sensitive clit against his groin. The bedroom was already filled with the musky aroma of their sex. It mixed with Mark's scent and their sweat, sending her arousal to the edge. Each stroke rubbed the sweet spot inside her, and she hovered ever so close to orgasm. He lifted her legs so they were over his shoulders. It sent his cock deeper into her cunt, and she went wild with pleasure. She raked her nails across his back, urging him to fuck her harder, faster, anything to make her come.

"I need it, Mark! Make me come! Fuck me hard!"

Mark reached between them and lightly pinched her clit. Her body went taut, and she screamed Mark's name as she tumbled over. Her climax blazed from her cunt and ran like quicksilver through her veins. He groaned and froze above her with a final thrust, his expression intense.

"Fuck, baby. Aw, fuck."

He collapsed on top of her, his breath coming in gasps. She clung to him, their bodies covered in sweat, sticky with her juices. It was raunchy and hot, and she loved it. He rolled away and discreetly disposed of the condom before pulling her into his arms with a smile.

"I think we're going to need a shower before we go dancing, sweetheart. You're all sweaty."

Becca ran her hand down his muscled, sweaty chest. "Only if you shower with me, you big stud."

Mark laughed. "You're the woman for me, baby. I'm hooked."

So was she. And she liked it.

Chapter 13

The Party was packed with people, and the beat from the music could be felt even through the chair Becca was sitting on. She had dragged Mark out on the dance floor despite Travis's warnings about lack of rhythm and found Mark could more than keep a beat. He was a good dancer, and they had soon dirty danced their way through "Tuff Enuff," "Dress You Up," and "You Dropped a Bomb on Me." "Tainted Love" was currently playing, but she needed something cool to drink more than she needed to grind against Mark's hunky body.

A body she had assaulted one more time in the shower. His skillful hands and tongue had her screaming his name. Their pants and moans of pleasure had echoed off the tile walls and had fueled their lovemaking until both of them could barely move. In fact, it was a testament to Mark's physical conditioning that he was here dancing with her now. He had certainly put in a full day's work in the sex department.

"Here you guys are! I wasn't sure I'd find you in this crowd."

Becca felt a tingle as Travis leaned forward and brushed her lips with his before doing the same to Mark. She hadn't realized how much she had missed being with both her men until she finally had them with her again. She tugged Travis into the chair next to hers.

"Where have you been? Mark and I have been having a great time, but I want to dance with you, too."

Travis squeezed her hand. "I want to dance with you, too, baby. Did you miss me?"

"A little. I had this big stud to keep me busy."

Travis laughed and signaled the waitress. "He is a big stud, isn't he? Did you two have a little fun tonight before you came dancing?"

Mark waggled his eyebrows. "That's her new nickname for me. Let's just say we were late. Very late. This woman is insatiable."

"That's why she's our woman. I'm glad you two were having fun while I was working. It was worth it, though. I learned some very interesting things about Randall the rat."

They had to lean their heads close together to hear Travis.

"I learned quite a bit about our guy. Seems he lost just about everything when the real estate bust happened. He had been overextended even before that, teetering on the edge of collapse anyway. When the market went, well, he pretty much lost everything."

Mark's brow knitted. "That was quite a while ago. What has he been doing since then?"

Travis shook his head. "That's the crux of this, I imagine. Apparently, our Randall doesn't like to live like the *little people*. He likes to live large, so to speak. He's been riding the line between lawful and unlawful for a few years now, taking part in some questionable investment deals with even more questionable business partners. I was able to find out he's being investigated by federal officials for RICO offenses. He needs a better class of friends. They don't have him yet, but they're close. It's only a matter of time before he's wearing an orange jumpsuit."

Becca sat back in amazement. "Poor Addie! Her nephew is a criminal. We have to tell her. He must be desperate and trying to get her money."

Travis nodded grimly. "I think so. I'll do what I can to make sure he can't touch any of her accounts. Do Mark and I have permission to worry about you now?"

Becca looked at Travis's serious expression. He really was worried.

"Why are you worried about me? I don't have what Randall wants."

"Yes, you do. Addie trusts you. He'll want to isolate her from people who care about her. That includes you."

"That includes a lot of people. That's how Plenty is."

"True, and that's the advantage we have over him. He won't expect the town to pull together and keep an eye on you and Addie."

Everything inside of Becca rebelled at the thought of having to be taken care of. However, she could see the wisdom in watching over Addie and, maybe just a little, herself.

"We definitely need to watch Addie, but I'm fine. I've seen Randall's type before. He's a coward. I can handle him."

Mark grabbed her hand. "I agree, baby. But cowards can be dangerous, too. We're going to have to tell Ryan what Trav found out. He'll sleep easier if he knows we're keeping an eye out for you. Unless you want to spend more time with Deputy Jason?"

Travis grabbed her other hand. "No, she does not. She's not spending any more time with her high school boyfriend."

Becca giggled. "Somebody's jealous. I like it."

"He just needs to find his own woman. We can take care of this one."

Becca ran her foot up Travis's leg and watched his eyes go wide in surprise.

"You men take care of me like no one else. Wanna do it again?"

Before Travis could answer, Justin Reynolds, the owner of the club, walked up to their table with a wide smile.

"Becca! I'm so glad you finally made it to my club. Are you having a good time?"

Justin was tall and handsome, with dirty-blond hair that brushed his collar and a body to die for. If she wasn't head over heels for Mark and Travis, she might have been interested.

"Yes, I am. I'd like you to meet my boyfriends, Dr. Mark Miller and Travis Andrews. They moved to Plenty recently, just like you. Guys, this is Justin Reynolds, the owner of this club."

The men shook hands, and Justin's mouth twisted into a smile. "Boyfriends, huh? Looks like I'm too late. And actually, I'm just half owner. My friend Linc Davis owns half, also. He was my manager while I was in the business."

Becca looked around. "I haven't met him yet. Is he here?"

Justin scanned the crowd. "Somewhere around here. He travels back and forth a lot. You'll meet him eventually."

Travis put a possessive arm around Becca. "So what made you decide to live in Plenty? It's probably a lot smaller and quieter than you're used to."

Justin grinned. "That's why I like it. I actually grew up in a small town. This feels like home. Plus this town is…open-minded. I was looking for a place to put down roots that doesn't judge."

Mark smiled. "Well, you certainly found the right town."

"I think I have. I want you to have a great time tonight, Becca. Everything is on the house."

Becca started to protest, but Justin held his hand. "This Eighties Night was your idea, and it's been a huge hit. Plus, I know you've been talking us up at your salon. People have told me they found out about the place from you."

Becca laughed. "This is Plenty, Justin. They would have found out anyway."

"I just want you to know I'm going to return the favor. I wouldn't let anyone say anything bad about you."

"Thank you. That's really sweet."

Something caught Justin's eye. "Listen, I'm needed at the bar. Have a great time tonight. And I meant what I said, Becca. No one will bad-mouth you when I'm around."

Justin hurried off, leaving Becca puzzled. "That was strange."

Travis took a drink of his beer. "I'll say. He was flirting with our woman."

Becca rolled her eyes. "Oh, please. He was just being nice. What was strange is what he said about not letting anyone bad-mouth me. Don't you think that's strange?"

Mark shrugged. "Maybe he's the protective type. I don't think he needs to worry about it. What could anyone say about you that's bad anyway? You're damn near perfect. How did you meet him?"

"Like I meet everyone in town. I cut his hair. I have the only hair salon in Plenty, remember? If they don't drive to Tampa or Orlando, then they don't have much choice but to patronize the Snip and Sing. And I'm not perfect. Nowhere near."

Mark leaned forward and gave her a sweet kiss. "You're perfect for us, then."

Travis tugged her out of her chair and toward the dance floor. "I want to dance with the most beautiful woman in Plenty."

Becca laughed as he pulled her close and started to move to the music. The song was "At This Moment," and it was one of her favorites. Travis pressed his warm body close to hers, and they moved slowly, synchronously, to the sad song. She felt his hand move up and down her back, and he suddenly stopped, lifting her chin to look into his eyes. She had never seen him look so serious, nor so determined.

"Fuck caution. Becca, I love you."

Travis's voice was thick with emotion. Becca's own throat tightened. His feelings were clearly on display. She licked her lips nervously. This was no time to wimp out. Every dream she ever had was coming true.

"I love you, too. And I love Mark, too."

Travis smiled, and some of the tension seemed to ease from his body. He waved at Mark to come over. Mark joined them, crowding her back and nuzzling her neck.

"What's going on here?"

Travis pulled Mark forward for a kiss. "I told Becca I love her, and she said she loves us back. That only leaves you who hasn't said it."

Mark's eyes widened, and then his face split into a big grin.

"Hell yes, I love you, Becca. You make everything complete. We're a family, baby."

Becca felt the tears welling in her eyes. "I'd given up, you know. I'd given up on finding something like this."

Mark traced her jaw with gentle fingers. "So had we, frankly. That's what makes this so special. We found what we hoped for but had given up on. We won't ever take it for granted. We're going to show you every day how much we love you."

Becca nodded. "I will, too. I promise. Can we go home now? I want to be with you. Both of you."

The men exchanged a look. Travis pushed back a stray hair from her face.

"Are you saying what we think you're saying?"

Becca started tugging them toward the door. "Yes, I want both of you at the same time. Please."

Mark laughed. "You never have to say *please* to get us to make love to you. It's our pleasure. Now let's get you home, my dick's hard already."

Becca shook her head. "You sweet talker. Let's see what we can do about that hard dick."

* * * *

Travis scooped her up in his arms and carried her from the car to the bedroom. It had been hard not to speed home from the club, but they had the rest of their lives to be together. This night was just the first of so many nights they would have as a family. Maybe someday, they could add on to their family, if Becca was willing. He would love to be a father. But tonight, first things first. He dropped her down on the bed with a grin.

"Last one naked gets a spanking."

Clothes started flying, but Becca was the last one undressed. She gave him a cute pout.

"It's not fair. I have more clothes to take off. The bra was especially difficult."

Travis turned to Mark. "What do you think? Should we show her some mercy?"

Mark grinned. "Fuck, no. She'd just do something else to misbehave. She loves getting spanked. Don't you, baby?"

Becca's face had turned a delicate pink. "Yes, I do. But only if you guys do it."

Mark pulled her to a standing position by the bed. "I don't see anyone else around here, do you? Looks like we'll be doing the spanking. Over Travis's knees, sweetie."

Becca put her hands on her hips and gave Mark a look of defiance. "That's it? Just assume the position? No foreplay? No buildup?"

Mark crossed his muscular arms across his chest. "Did you hear that, Trav? Our woman wants some foreplay. Maybe she's not wet yet."

Travis couldn't stop his smirk as he ran his fingers through her pussy. It was dripping with cream. He held up his glistening fingers.

"She's pretty wet for someone asking for foreplay. But if she wants it, then that's what we do."

He gently pushed her back on the bed, lying along one side with Mark on the other. Travis leaned down and captured her lips with his. She tasted like the Cherry Coke she loved to drink. He swirled his tongue in the warm cavern of her mouth. Her tongue played with his, stroking until his cock was hard and leaking pre-cum. He ruthlessly pushed back his own arousal. This was about sealing their love and commitment tonight, not about his own pleasure.

He lifted his head reluctantly, and Mark took his place. He caressed her generous breasts, pinching at the berry-colored nipples until they stood at attention. Becca moved restlessly under them, making small sounds from her throat. Mark started kissing his way down her neck, and Travis knew his destination. He shadowed Mark's actions, and they both reached a rosy nipple at the same time. They each licked and sucked until Becca was mewling and tugging on their hair, not to pull them away but to push them closer. He gave Mark a sign and began to nibble his way south, dipping his tongue in her belly button on the way to her pretty pussy.

He pushed her thighs apart, sticky from her arousal. He traced the folds of her cunt with his finger while Mark played with her breasts with his fingers and mouth. Becca looked to be in heaven. Her eyes were closed, her skin flushed, and her lips were parted as she panted and moaned. He smiled as he pressed two fingers inside her sopping pussy. Her body jerked and she moaned louder this time, her breathing getting ragged.

"Please, Travis, please fuck me!"

Her voice was strained and her pussy clamped down on his fingers. He shook his head.

"Sorry, baby. You asked for foreplay and a spanking, and that's what you're going to get. But I will take a little mercy on you."

Travis hooked his fingers and rubbed the sweet spot inside her while leaning down to tease her swollen clit with his tongue. Becca gushed more cream on his fingers, and he knew she was close to going over. He worked his tongue in firm licks, and she went off like a rocket. Her cunt squeezed his fingers, honey dripped on his hands, and her body went taut. Mark worked on her nipples while he worked her clit, tasting her sweet cream, until she was still and limp underneath them. She looked so fucking beautiful when she came. Travis's cock was screaming for satisfaction. He couldn't stop himself from reaching down and stroking it while his woman came back to earth. He groaned in frustration as her eyes opened and zeroed in on his straining dick, and she licked her lips with relish.

"Not now, baby. You've got a spanking coming."

* * * *

Becca quickly rolled over on the bed, presenting her bottom to her two delighted men. She couldn't wait to feel their firm hands spanking her ass. She wasn't about to pretend she didn't want it. She wanted it badly.

A hand came down sharply on her ass cheek, almost making her jump. The heat spread from her ass to her pussy, and she couldn't hold back the moan that escaped from her lips. Another hand came down on her other cheek, sending pleasure waves from the point of impact up her spine. Mark and Travis each took a side and in perfect rhythm took turns spanking her ass. Her bottom was on fire and her cunt was dripping as she rubbed her clit against the sheets, trying to get some relief. She groaned in frustration when the spanking stopped and she was rolled over on the bed, her sore ass rubbing on the sheets.

"I wasn't done yet, why did you stop?"

Mark chuckled. "You're the only woman I know who pouts about getting a spanking and then pouts because it's over too soon. My hand hurts, woman."

Becca laughed and reclined on the bed. The men leaned forward, but she held up her hand.

"Stop. I want to watch you two a little. It's hot."

Travis ran his hands up Mark's muscular chest.

"I don't have any problem with that. But we're fucking you together tonight. That's not negotiable."

Travis pulled Mark into his arms, and Becca watched, mesmerized, as their lips and tongues met in a scorching kiss. She couldn't tear away from the feast of gorgeous man flesh on display for her eyes, and her eyes only. Their bodies were pressed close, their mouths devouring each other. Mark's hand reached between them to stroke Travis's hard cock. Travis hissed with pleasure.

"Isn't it beautiful, Becca? Doesn't Trav have the most beautiful cock?"

Becca nodded. "You both do. Lick it."

Mark grinned. "Your wish is my command."

He leaned down and licked Travis's cock from balls to tip several times. Becca was amazed at how Travis's body shook from the pleasure.

"Lick him, too."

Travis pushed Mark down to the bed and did more than that. He licked and kissed a trail from Mark's lips, down his neck, across his chest and abs, all the way to his cock and balls. Mark was moaning as Travis worked his tongue around the mushroom head of Mark's cock, his fingers twisting in Travis's silky brown hair. Becca's nipples were painfully tight and her pussy was creaming as she watched Travis pleasure Mark. Mark tugged at Travis's hair.

"Fuck, if you keep that up, this is going to be over before it starts."

Mark's voice was hoarse and gravelly. Travis sat up with a satisfied smile.

"I guess I'd just have to get you hard again. What a job."

Mark sat up and pulled his lover close for another kiss.

"I love you, babe."

"Yeah, I love you, too. Now let's fuck our woman. I don't want her getting the idea she's in charge around here. I do want her to get the idea of how much we love her."

Mark snagged her ankle and pulled her toward the end of the bed so he could get into position while Travis grabbed condoms and lube from the nightstand. Her pulse hummed as she anticipated having both her men fucking her at the same time. She trailed her finger down the center of Mark's chest.

"You know I want it hard and hot, right?"

Mark eased back on the bed, sliding his head up to the top, and patted his stomach in invitation.

"Let's get inside you, babe, before you decide how hard you want it. The first time can be uncomfortable at first, and we don't want you to be too sore tomorrow."

Becca didn't want to be sore tomorrow either, but she was practically panting to have her men fuck her. Mark slipped on a condom and tugged her on top of him. She giggled as the rough hair on his legs tickled the sensitive skin on the inside her of thighs. They were both so sexy, and she couldn't help reaching out and running her hands all over his chest and shoulders, loving the way his hard muscles and smooth skin felt under her palms.

He returned the favor, skimming his hands up her rib cage and under her heavy breasts before tugging her down until her nipples dangled over his mouth. He tortured each nipple in turn with his lips and tongue until she was grinding her pussy against his hard cock. He laughed at her desperate response.

"I think our woman needs a cock inside her, stat."

Travis rolled his eyes and helped Becca get into position on top of Mark.

"Dr. Feelgood likes to use medical humor sometimes. You'll get used to it."

Becca closed her eyes and let the pleasure wash over her as she lowered herself onto Mark's stiff cock. Each ridge rubbed sensitive spots in her cunt, and she groaned when he was seated to the hilt. She felt so full, her pussy stretched to accommodate him. Nothing felt as delicious as Mark's and Travis's cocks.

"It feels so good. Mark's dick fills me up. God, I love it."

Travis swept her hair off her neck and kissed the sensitive spot there.

"I love it when Mark fucks me. Open your eyes, pretty girl, and see the look on his face. You can see he loves being inside you, too."

Becca opened her eyes, and Mark did have a look of complete pleasure on his face. He pulled her down on his chest, nuzzling her hair and playing with her nipples. Travis caressed her bottom.

"I'm going to fill you up here. You're going to be so full of cock, the feeling is going to be out of this world. Just relax for me, babe. Let Mark distract you."

Becca tried to relax and concentrate on Mark's hands instead of Travis's. She jumped a little when she felt the cold lube trickle down her ass crack, but then Travis's warm fingers were rubbing her back hole.

"Breathe."

Becca exhaled slowly as Travis's fingers breached her ass. A second finger was quickly added. She felt a zing of pleasure as his fingers found sensitive nerves she hadn't known existed until she met these men. His fingers scissored and worked, stretching her until he was sure she could take him. She cried out when he pulled his fingers from her.

"No! Travis, I need it."

He ran his hand up and down her back in a soothing motion.

"I know you do, baby. I know what you need. You need a cock in your ass, don't you? I'm going to give you one. The time has come for us to all be together."

She heard the crinkle of a condom wrapper, and then the blunt end of his cock pressed against her back hole insistently. Her body resisted for a moment, and then the tight ring of muscles gave way. She felt the brief bite of pain she loved so much and the burn which quickly turned to a dark pleasure. She hadn't expected to enjoy it this much. His cock was sending frissons of pleasure through her body and straight to her pussy. She could feel her cunt tighten on Mark's cock and was rewarded with his moan of ecstasy.

"Fuck, Trav. Her pussy just clamped down on my cock. Let's get to fucking soon. I don't know how much longer I can hold back."

"I'm almost in, babe. Hold on one more minute."

Travis pressed relentlessly into her tight hole until he had given her everything he had to give. She was panting, her body shiny with sweat. She was completely stuffed with cock, and nothing could have prepared her for how it felt. Travis's cock felt a hundred times better than the plug. The plug had been cold and hard. Travis's cock was hard, hot, and pulsing. She knew now why Cassie and Jillian were always smiling. She wanted this every day for the rest of her life.

"Do it."

Her men knew exactly what to do. Travis pulled out before slowly thrusting back in, his balls slapping her ass as he drove in to the hilt. As Travis pistoned in, Mark pulled out, only to slam into her as Travis pulled out again. Every single second of her fucking she was filled with cock. They played her body between them like a fine instrument. She was lost to the pleasure and feelings, her senses fully engaged. She could hear their pants and her own urgent voice. She could smell the heavy scent of sex that hung in the air. When Travis pulled her back against his chest, she tasted his seductive kiss, his flavor uniquely male. She could see Mark's face, a mask of concentration as he tried to hold back, to draw out the pleasure as long as they could. Finally, she could feel their hair-roughened skin against her own, rubbing against her each time they moved together.

Their movements became more urgent, and her body grew taut as the pleasure inside her built. She was on the edge, and she knew just one more stroke would send her into orgasm. Mark reached between them and gave her swollen, sensitive clit the attention it had been screaming for. At the same time, Travis nipped at the sensitive spot on her neck just where it met her shoulder. The twin sensations sent her over, and she shattered into a million pieces. The pleasure was so intense it was almost painful, yet she never wanted it to end.

Mark thrust one more time and froze. His body went rigid, and she could see the veins of his neck clearly as he muttered a filthy word. She could feel his cock pulsing inside of her, and it sent her into another wave of pleasure she hadn't anticipated. Travis's hands bit into her hips as he also climaxed. She could feel his hot seed spurting, filling the condom. It seemed to last forever, and then finally it was over. They collapsed in a heap of arms and legs, sticky with sweat and sex.

They lay there for a long time, no one speaking, just enjoying the intimacy of what they had just shared. Becca had never felt closer to anyone in her life than she did at this moment with these two men she loved so much. She protested when she felt them move and the men start to get up from the bed.

"No, stay here with me."

Travis gave her a quick, sweet kiss.

"We'll be right back, babe. We need to take care of these condoms."

The light in the bathroom went on, and she closed her eyes and let herself drift on the edge of sleep. She was startled when she felt a warm washcloth between her legs.

"What—"

"Easy there, sweetheart. We're just cleaning you up, and then we can all cuddle and go to sleep."

Becca relaxed under Mark's caring ministrations. She had never felt so loved and cared for, protected even. Maybe being protected by these men wouldn't be as annoying as being protected by her big brothers.

"You have a very witchy smile on your face, pretty girl. What are you thinking about?"

"That you're not as annoying as Ryan and Jack."

Mark barked with laughter. "I would hope that's the case. How about let's leave your brothers out of our bedroom? Deal?"

Mark cuddled Becca's front and Travis joined them, snuggling her back. She yawned, barely able to keep her eyes open.

"Deal. No Ryan or Jack in our bedroom. Ever."

Chapter 14

The insistent ring of the telephone brought Becca reluctantly awake. She propped one eye open as Mark grabbed the phone.

"Becca, honey, it's Ryan."

So much for keeping her brothers out of their bedroom. She reached for the phone with a grimace.

"This better be good, big brother."

"I wouldn't have called unless it was important. The salon was vandalized last night."

Becca sat up quickly, causing Mark and Travis to look alarmed. She knew she was probable scaring them, but at the moment she was too pissed off to care.

"What? Vandalized? How much damage? Shit, I'll be right there."

Becca was already pushing the covers back and levering out of bed. Her hair salon was her pride and joy, and someone had damaged it.

"Easy, sis. Have Travis or Mark drive you, okay? I don't want you driving if you're this upset."

Becca held the phone in one hand while she dragged her panties and skirt up with the other.

"I'm not upset, Ryan. I'm pissed. I'll be there in ten."

Becca slammed the phone on the cradle and only then noticed her men had also started to get dressed. Travis pulled a T-shirt over his head and then stayed her hand as she tried to drag on her blouse.

"Stop. You can't wear that. Let me get you some gym shorts and a T-shirt of mine, and you have some flip-flops here you can wear."

Becca was about to ask him what he was talking about but then took a good look at herself in the mirror. She was wearing her sexy outfit from last night. What was hot for an evening out with her boys would look tarty in the cold light of morning. She didn't want to show up at her shop with Ryan dressed like a hooker. She sighed in defeat.

"Okay. I guess I would look pretty ridiculous. Thanks."

Mark pulled her close for a hug. "Relax, babe. We're here for you, okay? You're not alone. We're a family now."

Becca felt tears prick the backs of her eyes. "I love you both so much."

"And we love you. Let's get you dressed and get out of here so we can see what happened."

* * * *

Becca had to hold back her tears as she took in the damage to her beloved salon. The front window had been shattered by a large rock thrown at it. On the door, the word *whore* was spray-painted in a crimson red. Inside wasn't much better. The vandals has apparently crawled through the broken window and proceeded to pull shelves down, scattering products all over the floor and knocking over tables and chairs. The inside walls were spray-painted with letters three feet tall, spelling *Bitch*. And to top it all off, every mirror in the place was cracked. Becca didn't even want to think about how many years of bad luck that was.

"It can all be fixed."

Mark's arm was warm and solid around her shoulders. She let herself lean against him, thankful for his strength.

"I know. But it still pisses me off anyway. Why would someone do this?"

As the town woke up, the scene attracted quite a crowd. Becca was grateful that Travis and Mark had insisted she take an extra minute to wash last night's melted makeup from her face and pull her hair back in a ponytail. She didn't look glamorous in Travis's gray running shorts and dark-blue T-shirt, but she at least looked clean and neat.

Ryan pulled his cell phone from his ear and gave her a grim look.

"I had my deputies checking all over town. There doesn't appear to be any other damage anywhere. Only here. The insurance adjuster was already here. He'll get a copy of all the crime-scene photos. You should be completely covered."

"Terrific. What did I do to piss someone off like this?"

Travis pushed his way through debris and started righting the tables and chairs, noting the damage to the upholstery and table finishes.

"Did you have anyone complain lately? Any unsatisfied customers?"

Becca rubbed her temples. "No. I make sure everyone is happy with their hair. In fact, things have been going great lately. No complaints at all."

Mike Parks pushed his way into the shop and gave Becca a big hug.

"Oh, honey, I came as soon as I heard. We'll get this place cleaned up before you know it. Don't you worry, okay?"

Becca felt the familiar rush of love as she looked at her father's worried face. It appeared he had dragged Steve and Ellie with him, and their expressions were just as concerned.

"I'm not worried. I know everything can be replaced or fixed. I'm insured, and they've already been here. I'm just pissed off that someone did this. I'm sorry about your karaoke equipment. I think it's a write-off."

Mike Parks kept his music equipment in the back of the salon. He loved karaoke and it was great entertainment for the customers. It was the reason she had named the salon The Snip and Sing.

"My only concern is that you are okay. We can buy new karaoke equipment. I can't buy another daughter."

Ellie came forward and handed her a cup of coffee. "Steve and I stopped at the diner. We thought you might need some coffee."

Becca gave her a grateful smile and sipped at the hot coffee. "This is just what I needed. Thank you, Ellie."

"Becca! Becca! Dear, are you all right?"

Becca looked past Ellie and gave a fond smile. Two of her favorite customers were pushing through the crowd and into her shop. Estelle and Jane were sisters and members of the Ladies Auxiliary. Both retired and widowed, the ladies were in their seventies but didn't look a day over sixty. Neck deep in civic affairs, they knew everyone and everything that went on in Plenty.

"I'm fine, Estelle. Just the shop was damaged."

Estelle and Jane looked around the shop with disgust and determination. Becca knew that look well. The ladies were cooking up something. Jane pulled out her cell phone.

"I'm going to call the other ladies, and we'll get a crew in here to clean this up."

Becca protested. "We can handle this, Jane. That's so sweet, but we can get this cleaned up."

Jane gave her a no-nonsense look. "We'll help. You're one of us, dear, and we care for our own. Heavens, you're always doing something for Plenty, whether it's the meal program, sponsoring a Little League team, volunteering at the hospital, or any of the other hundred things you do for this community. It's time for Plenty to help you."

Becca was speechless. She hadn't realized anyone had been paying attention. She hadn't done those things for the attention, of course. She truly loved helping people. It was what she, Ryan, and Jack all had in common. They all three had a deep sense of civic responsibility. But she was amazed to hear that her efforts hadn't gone unnoticed.

Travis put his arm around her shoulders and pulled her close. "She is amazing, isn't she, ma'am? Mark and I are very proud of her."

"As well you should be, young man. Our Becca is very special. I hope you plan to treat her right?"

Becca felt her face get warm as she thought about how right she had been treated the night before. Travis just smiled easily at Jane's nosy inquiry. "She is special, and our intentions are honorable, I assure you."

His answer must have satisfied her, as she began dialing numbers on her cell phone and talking animatedly into the phone.

"The town loves you, pretty girl. Mark and I better mind our p's and q's."

Becca nodded and felt the moisture well up in her eyes. She was overwhelmed by the outpouring of support. The people outside the shop had started to stream in with brooms and trash bags, sweeping and cleaning up debris. Dr. Steve had brought his toolbox, and shelves were already being rehung on the walls. She stood for a moment, overcome with thankfulness at living in this wonderful town.

"This is just—"

Her voice was choked, and Travis hugged her closer.

"It's just this town trying to show you some of what you give them every day. You're not just Ryan and Jack's little sister and a good little girl, babe. You're Becca Parks, business owner and pillar of the community. You're your own person."

She realized what Travis said was true. All along she had felt like the town saw her in only one way—the good little sister to Ryan and Jack. She had no doubt that at one time this had been true. But it was clear it was years ago and long past. She could see in people's eyes they respected her. How long had she been blind to the changes? It didn't matter. She knew it now.

She looked up at Travis and gave him a smile. The day wasn't a total loss.

"I certainly am. We better get this place cleaned up. I have a full docket of appointments starting Monday morning."

"You give the orders and we're the muscle, baby."

Becca let her gaze wander up and down Travis and Mark's impressive physiques.

"Yes, you are."

* * * *

Becca fell back into the couch and surveyed the shop. It wasn't perfect. Some of the chairs would need to be repaired, and she would need to replace the retail products she sold, but it was sufficient for her to open Monday morning. Somehow, Estelle and Jane had convinced a mirror supplier from Orlando to drive over on a Saturday and replace every broken mirror in the place. They were formidable women.

"I can't believe we got it cleaned up. Even the paint is gone from the walls."

The walls were now freshly painted a modern shade of bluish gray. Mark looked up from where he was wiping down a counter.

"The whole town pitched in. It just shows what can happen when everyone works together. Shame about the front window, but the installer said it would only take a few days to get that custom size."

Travis fell back on the couch next to her. "Those storefront windows have to be custom cut. The plywood will have to do until then."

Becca scowled at the wood covering her front window. Until it was replaced, it would be a constant reminder of what had happened.

The bell over the door rang, and Ryan strode into the shop and looked around with a grin.

"Holy hell, it's all cleaned up. I should have known it would be. Becca's like a tiny drill sergeant when she has a project."

Becca turned her scowl on her oldest brother.

"A drill sergeant? You have a lot of nerve. You're the one usually shouting orders around here."

"That so? Well, I'm about to do it again."

Becca held up her hand.

"Save your breath. Mark and Travis have already been reading me the riot act about being safe and staying away from Randall the rat. I assume you think he's responsible for this?"

Ryan gave her a challenging look. "Don't you? I'm guessing he was also responsible for the mailboxes at your condo."

Becca sighed. "Probably. I can't imagine what he would get out of this. Seems like a really stupid thing to do."

Mark shook his head. "I met this guy, and he doesn't seem real bright to me. Have you talked to him, Ryan?"

"No, the Orlando authorities went to his home to question him and it looks like he's cleared out. The house is in foreclosure anyway. He would have been thrown out in a few weeks."

"You don't think he's violent, do you?" Mark asked.

Ryan shrugged. "From the pansy-ass things he's done so far, I would say no. He seems passive-aggressive, though, which means he might want to damage more property. Maybe your home or car. I'm going to put my men driving by your condo and the shop on a regular basis, and don't bother to protest, little sister. You won't talk me out of this."

"I'm not even going to try."

Travis popped open a soda and handed it to her. "You'll stay with us until Randall is found. And you won't talk us out of that, either."

Becca slipped her hand into his larger one. "I think that sounds like a plan. A plan I like."

Ryan rolled his eyes. "Well, I can see I'm completely unneeded here. I'm going to get home to my woman now before I end up in the doghouse again. Lock up the store behind you, Becca."

"Got it, big brother. Say hi to Jillian for me."

Mark came and sat on her other side, wrapping an arm around her shoulders. "You're going to love staying with us, pretty girl. Maybe we can convince you to stay even after Randall is found."

Becca ran her hands up their muscular thighs. "I'm ready to be convinced. But first, we need to see Addie. I don't want her hearing about this from anyone but me."

Travis hopped to his feet. "Then we better hurry. The way news travels in this town, we'll need all the head start we can get. I'll drive."

* * * *

"Becca! What a nice surprise. And you've brought your young men, too."

Becca smiled at Addie. She was looking more like herself every day. Soon, Becca wouldn't have the excuse of delivering meals to see her.

"I did bring Mark and Travis today. You remember Mark from the other day, don't you?"

"Of course I do. I'm not that old, no matter what this piece of paper may say."

Becca forgot all about introducing Travis. "What piece of paper?"

Addie picked up a thick stack of papers from the end table and waved them with an air of disgust.

"This piece of paper. I was served with papers yesterday. My grandnephew Randall wants me declared incompetent."

Travis sat next to Addie on the couch and gave her a charming smile.

"Miss Addie, I'm Travis Andrews. I'm an attorney. Would you mind if I took a look at those papers?"

Addie handed them over with relief. "It's nice to meet you, Travis. Please go right ahead. A lot of legal gobbledygook from what I can see. Maybe you can make heads or tails of them."

"Addie, why didn't you call me yesterday when you got these papers?"

"You're so sweet, Becca dear, but you have your own life to worry about. I knew I'd see you this coming week. Nothing was going to change between now and then, so why bother you?"

Becca sighed in frustration. "You never bother me, Addie. I care about you like my own family." Becca patted Addie's hand. "Can I make you some tea?"

"That would be nice. I want to sit and get to know your young men. They certainly are handsome."

Addie did love handsome young men. Becca had seen a picture of Addie's late husband, and he had been quite a good-looking man.

Becca kept busy in the kitchen, straining to hear the quiet conversation in the other room. By the time she returned, the three looked like old friends. Addie was beaming and seemed completely relaxed despite the threat hanging over her head. Becca placed the tray on the coffee table and started pouring the tea, casting a questioning glance at Travis and Mark.

Travis handed the teacup to Addie. "We just told Addie what I found out about Randall."

Becca chewed on her lower lip. "I'm so sorry, Addie. I wish Travis had found out something different."

Addie shook her head with a sad smile. "I'm sorry, too. I'm mostly sorry that Randall has decided to harass a nice young woman such as yourself. Your men told me what he did to your hair salon."

"We don't know for sure it's Randall."

Addie tutted. "I'm sure it is. Even as a child, Randall was spiteful. He always wanted his own way. Sadly, that trait has carried itself into adulthood. You shouldn't have to worry about such things just because we're friends."

"Your friendship means more to me than this nonsense with Randall," Becca said fiercely.

Mark squeezed her hand. "We're going to end this nonsense with Randall as soon as possible."

"Addie, will you let me represent you in the competency hearing next week?" Travis asked.

Addie sipped at her tea. "Should I be worried? I would hope it's obvious that I have my wits about me."

Travis shook his head. "No, you shouldn't be. But I'd like to be there to navigate the legal maze you may encounter. It would be my pleasure."

Addie looked thoughtful but finally nodded. "Okay, if you think it will help. I don't mind having a handsome young man at my side when I go out. As long as Becca doesn't mind sharing. I wouldn't want her to get jealous."

Becca laughed. "I don't mind sharing, Addie. And I'll try not to get too jealous."

Travis poured Addie more tea. "It's settled then. I'll let the court know I'm the attorney of record. We'll get this out of the way so you can concentrate on getting better."

Becca leaned forward and whispered in Travis's ear, "You're my hero today."

Travis whispered back, "Anything for you, pretty girl. Anything."

Chapter 15

Becca pushed her pot roast around on her plate as she listened to Cassie and Jillian discuss the rehearsal dinner. They were planning an outdoor barbecue at Zach and Chase's horse farm, and they were discussing if the weather would hold. She tried to take part in the conversation, but she was exhausted and her stomach was upset. It had been since the day before, and she hadn't eaten anything out of the ordinary. She would just be glad when Addie's hearing was over and Randall was found. Things would go back to normal.

"Are you going to eat that or just play with it?" Cassie peered at Becca's plate.

Becca sighed and dropped her fork on the plate. "I'm not hungry. For some reason my stomach is upset."

Cassie arched an eyebrow. "For some reason? How about some asshole wrecked your shop and is trying to get control of Addie's money? That's a pretty good reason to be nauseous, if you ask me. Maybe you should have some chocolate cake. That always makes me feel better."

Becca's stomach lurched, and she pressed her hand over her mouth. Jillian's eyes widened.

"You're not kidding, are you? Geez, Becca, maybe you should be home in bed. Do you want us to drive you back to Mark and Travis's?"

"I'm not that sick. I just need a Zantac or something. Besides, the house is empty. You know Mark and Travis are playing poker with your men tonight."

Jillian speared a piece of asparagus. "The men want us to stay with you until they get home, you know."

Becca rolled her eyes. "I know. Mark and Travis are protective. I'm humoring them, if you want to know the truth."

Cassie laughed. "We're all humoring our men, if the truth be known."

Jillian waved at a pretty young woman who had come into the diner. "Ava! Come on over and join us!"

A tiny, dark-haired woman turned and smiled, heading toward their table.

"Hi, Jillian. I didn't expect to see you here tonight."

Jillian patted the seat next to her in the booth. "We come here every Monday night for a girl's night out. Ava, these are my friends Cassie Ames and Becca Parks. Girls, this is Ava Bryant. She's Mark's nurse. She just moved here from Chicago."

Becca felt a twinge of jealousy. The young woman was very pretty. She tried to remember if Mark had ever mentioned his nurse.

"I arrived just a few days ago. I've been Mark's nurse for years. When he told me he was moving to a small town in Florida, I thought he had lost his mind. But just after a few days here, I can see what attracted him. I'm excited about starting new here. And of course I've heard about you, Becca. Mark talks about you constantly. He loves you very much."

Becca felt instantly guilty for her jealousy. Ava seemed like a nice woman.

Becca gave her a welcoming smile. "I love him, too. Very much. Welcome to Plenty. You'll love it here. We'll make sure of that."

Cassie chuckled. "Just watch out for the men around here. Jillian and I were scooped up before we knew what had happened to us. There's just something about the men in Plenty. They're just so—"

"Manly," Jillian finished.

Becca grinned. "They are that. Sexy, too."

Ava gave a small smile and shook her head. "The very last thing I need is a man. I'm recently divorced. I wouldn't say that I have a positive view of male-female relationships. I'm looking forward to being on my own."

Jillian pushed her plate away. "I'm guessing the men in this town are going to have a hard time leaving you alone. They have a way of flying under the radar and sneaking into your heart. And bed."

"No one is going to be sneaking into my heart or my bed. I'm done with men. For good. I just want to live a quiet, simple life here in Plenty. No drama."

* * * *

Poker night at Ryan and Jack's was always a lively evening, and tonight was no exception. The men were joking and laughing while they kicked back with junk food, beers, and cigars.

"Dammit, smoke those things outside. Jillian will have my ass on a platter if she comes home and smells cigar smoke in the house."

Jack laughed at Ryan shooing the men out to the front porch. Ryan was always keeping Jack out of trouble with Jillian. Mark knew his little sister could be hell on wheels when her dander was up.

"Hey, Ryan. Can I talk to you?"

Mark was worried about the strain Becca seemed to be feeling. Although she had seemed more angry than upset about the damage to her shop, she had picked at her breakfast this morning and had dark circles under her eyes when she returned from work today. He and Travis didn't like her looking so fragile. The sooner Randall stopped harassing Becca the better.

Mark grabbed a slice of pizza and sat down next to Ryan and Jack. Ryan handed him a cold beer with a grimace.

"I know what you're going to ask. Randall's disappeared. Vanished. The good news is he doesn't seem to be a physical danger to anyone, just an asshole. If we're lucky, he may not even show up for Miss Addie's hearing."

Travis sat down next to them. "If I have my way, there won't even be a hearing."

Jack handed Travis a beer. "Can you do that?"

"I'm working on it. I'm starting to collect affidavits regarding Addie's competency. I'm hoping the judge will throw out the case as it's only Randall's word."

Ryan nodded. "I'd be willing to make a statement. Addie is a good woman and more sane than most people in Plenty."

"I'd be grateful. A statement from the town sheriff would go a long way."

Mark gave his lover an encouraging smile. If anyone could make this go away, it was Travis. He was a hell of a lawyer and just about the smartest man Mark had ever met. His cautious nature made sure he looked at all sides of a situation before acting. Of course, Travis had been fairly impetuous lately when it came to Becca. After all, it had been Travis who had said "I love you" first. Mark was still shocked about that. He had thought it would take a lot of cajoling to get him to admit it.

"Happy to do it. Now let's get dinner out of the way so we can play some cards. I'm feeling lucky tonight."

Jack cracked up. "You're always feeling lucky, bro."

Mark felt a tug on his sleeve and looked up in surprise. Travis was motioning him over to the back door in the kitchen. Mark followed him as they stepped outside. Despite the fact it was only the beginning of April, it was still quite warm at night.

"What's up, babe?"

Travis pulled him close, and his scent filled Mark's nostrils. He ran his hands down Travis's back and wondered for the thousandth time how he had gotten so lucky in his life to find this man so many years ago and now Becca to share their lives together.

"I'm worried about Becca. She looked terrible this morning. You would have thought she hadn't slept, but she slept like the dead last night. Then this morning she barely touches her breakfast. It's not like her. I know Ryan is doing his best, but I was thinking about using some of my law contacts and hiring a private investigator to find Randall. It won't be cheap, but I do think it will be effective."

Mark nodded. "I'm really worried about her, too. She seemed okay yesterday, but perhaps this is all just starting to wear on her nerves. As for the money, what's our money for anyway? I can't think of a better use for it than to care for our family. What happens if they find him?"

Travis shrugged. "Ryan gets to talk to him in an official capacity. He'll warn him to stay away from Becca and let him know that he's being watched. Right now he has no idea we suspect him."

"How can we not suspect him? Who else wants to harass Becca?"

"I know that and you know that, but he doesn't. He may think Becca has others who want to bother her. Who knows what he gains from this? I just want him to leave our woman alone."

"Me, too. Make your call then. If Ryan can't find him, maybe we can."

Travis nodded and stepped away, pulling his phone out of his pocket. He gave Mark a smile.

"I'll come inside in a minute. Tell the guys to go ahead and start without me."

* * * *

Zach and Chase's huge backyard was the perfect place for a wedding or even a wedding rehearsal. The large oak and maple trees provided plenty of shade, and Zach and Chase had set up tables and chairs with bright-red tablecloths loaded with finger food.

Cassie and Jillian were off making last-minute preparations for the wedding tomorrow, and Becca and Ellie had promised to hold down the fort at the rehearsal. The men had the grills going, Mike and Steve had fired up the brand-new karaoke equipment, and Jack was playing bartender. It was Jack who was also playing the clown. He presented both grooms with brand-new running shoes so they could run away from matrimony if they had cold feet. The men were having a good laugh over it.

"You think that's funny, do you?"

Jack whirled around and turned pale as he faced a very pissed-off-looking Jillian. She had her arms crossed over her chest and was tapping her foot.

"Fuck. Shit. Aw, honey, it was just a joke. I love you, baby."

Ryan shook his head. "Jack, for fuck's sake, am I going to spend the rest of my life getting you out of the doghouse?"

Jillian turned and started marching toward the house with Jack at her heels professing love and offering to marry her right this very minute. Becca would have thought Jillian was madder than hell if she hadn't glimpsed the smile playing around her lips right before she went into the house and slammed the door.

Becca wiped the tears from her eyes and her sides ached from laughing so hard. She really needed this night of fun. It had been a long week since her shop had been vandalized, but Randall the rat hadn't made any more appearances. Becca would have been surprised if he had, as she had him pegged as a great big pussy who would run from his own shadow. But the week was over and she was determined to put the entire incident behind her. It was Cassie, Zach, and Chase's weekend.

"Hey, pretty girl, what's got my little sister all fired up?"

Becca felt her heart flip in her chest as Mark and Travis walked toward her. She wondered if she would ever get over how handsome and sexy they were. Today, Mark was in blue jeans and a button-down shirt. His blond hair was slightly ruffled as if he had run his fingers through it at some point, which he probably had. He had a very stressful job even in a small town like Plenty.

Travis was still dressed in the suit he had worn to work this morning. The conservative dark-blue suit couldn't hide his muscular shoulders and flat abs. Becca licked her lips as she remembered how she had licked down those abs just this morning. Her tongue had licked a path all the way to his hard and very eager cock. She had sucked Travis's cock while Mark fucked her from behind, tugging on her hair and smacking her ass. It was just how she liked it—rough, raunchy, and dirty.

"Jack decided to get Zach and Chase a gag gift of running shoes, and let's just say after their history, Jillian didn't appreciate the joke."

Jack had been commitment shy when he first met Jillian, but his love for her was greater than his fear of settling down. They were all now happily engaged and planning a June wedding.

Mark chuckled. "I bet she didn't. Jack has no sense of self-preservation. Jillian's going to lead him by the nose for the rest of his life."

Becca quirked an eyebrow. "Is there anything wrong with that? Are you trying to say something?"

Mark looked surprised and then laughed. "Fuck, no, babe. I'm not trying to say anything. I'm happy to be led around by the nose by you from now to the end of time."

Travis rolled his eyes. "Nice save, Romeo."

"Think you would do better?"

"I wouldn't get myself into the situation in the first place. Think before you speak. You and Jack are more alike than you want to admit."

Travis was certainly the more cautious of her two men. The men were the perfect balance really. Travis, so careful and thoughtful. Mark, so playful and spontaneous. She had the best of both worlds.

They each took a seat next to her, and Travis lifted her fingers to his lips. She loved looking deeply into his brown eyes, so soft and soulful. She could get lost in them. Today they had sparks of gold in them. Travis was excited about something.

"I have news, babe. After several affidavits and meetings with the judge, the competency hearing for Addie has been dropped. I just got the word and stopped by Addie's on the way here to let her know."

Becca hesitated for only a second before letting out a whoop that got the attention of everyone in the backyard and maybe a few of the horses in the barn. She launched herself at Travis, hugging and kissing him and telling him what a stud attorney he was.

"Whoa, babe. I love the enthusiasm, but let's save it for later when we're alone."

Becca giggled as they drew a crowd. Her smile was a mile wide as she made the announcement.

"Ladies and gentlemen, Travis just got word that the competency hearing against Addie has been dropped! Randall the rat loses! Addie wins!"

Everyone started talking and asking questions at once. Travis did his best to answer them all, but it came down to one simple fact—Randall had no case.

Becca cuddled next to Travis. "You are one awesome attorney. I love you."

Mark gave a heavy sigh. "And I'm just chopped liver, huh, babe?"

Becca laughed at Mark's hangdog expression.

"I love you, too, you big stud. You're just as awesome."

Mark brightened and then ran his hand up her thigh.

"Well, in that case…"

Becca pushed his hand away. "Uh-uh, this is Cassie's night. We have to rehearse, eat, toast, and be merry. And remember, Jillian, Cassie, and myself are spending the night at Cassie and Jillian's condo."

Both men looked crestfallen. She was a little disappointed herself. She has gotten used to falling asleep between their warm, muscular bodies. She would have to console herself tonight with some fun with her girlfriends.

"It's just one night. I'll miss you both, too. But look at the bright side. You'll get to spend some time with each other. Don't you miss being alone?"

Becca held her breath as she waited for the answer. She shouldn't want them to say no, but she did. Her men looked confused, and then Travis grabbed her hand with a determined expression.

"Mark and I have been alone for fifteen years. Hell, we were alone in the car on the way over here. We can be alone pretty much anytime, if you want to know the truth. We want to be with you, Becca. We love being with you. There will be times when we'll be alone with each other and when you'll be alone with Mark or me. But the reason we want to be in this relationship is so we can all be together. I want to be very clear here. We don't miss or have nostalgic feelings for our time before you. We think being with you is better."

Becca sniffled, tears welling in her eyes. They couldn't be any more clear, and she hadn't even realized she needed to hear it.

"I think being with you is better, too. I wish I could go home with you tonight, but I promised Cassie. It's her last night as a single woman, and we have to give her a proper send-off."

Mark gave her a big grin. "As long as we get every other night, we can give up this one."

Becca hugged her men, breathing in their heady scents.

"All the other nights. Promise."

Chapter 16

"I guess we could order some pay-per-view porn."

Jillian rolled her eyes. It was obvious she found the idea distasteful. The three of them were relaxing in the living room of Cassie and Jillian's condo for Cassie's last night as a single woman. They were trying to decide how to spend the evening.

Cassie made a face. "Ick. It's so clinical. It's almost like a recipe. Take one big cock and shove it in. Pan camera to crotch shot. Thrust vigorously until female fakes orgasm. Male pulls out and shoots all over female. Female pretends to like it. Rinse and repeat."

Becca giggled. "Don't forget the cheesy music in the background. That's always very important."

"And the men are never very good looking. Can't they find a good-looking man who's well hung, too?" Jillian asked.

Cassie smiled. "Nope. Because the three of us cornered the market."

They all fell into peals of laughter. Jillian shook her head sadly.

"Let's face it. We've become boring and settled. We all might as well get married and have six kids."

Becca's eyebrows shot up. "Six kids? I don't want six kids. Two, maybe three would be okay."

Cassie sighed. "We're going to try and have a baby right away. There's no need to wait."

"You don't want to wait and have some time as newlyweds?" Becca asked.

Cassie shook her head. "We'll have time while I'm pregnant. Chances are I won't get pregnant right away anyhow."

Becca looked doubtful. "You don't know that. You could get pregnant right away. You could get pregnant when you least expect it."

"I wouldn't mind. What about you, Jillian? Are you, Ryan, and Jack going to try for a baby right away?"

Jillian shook her head. "We've decided to wait at least six months, maybe a year. Ryan wants to be able to get his schedule under control first. It will take that long to hire a couple more deputies and train them."

Jillian turned to Becca. "What about you? Do you want kids right away?"

Becca felt her face get warm. "I'm not even engaged yet. Why are you asking me about kids?"

Jillian grinned. "The way my brother and Travis look at you, you won't be single for long. You'll be married before the year's out."

Becca fiddled with the television remote. "I hope they want to marry me. I mean, I want to marry them. But they've never mentioned marriage. If they were marriage minded, wouldn't they have already married each other? There are states that would marry them."

Jillian looked thoughtful. "They've always been married in their hearts, I know that. Maybe they just never got around to it. But I can tell they're crazy about you. I can tell they're serious."

"I don't need to be married to be committed to them. It would just be nice. I guess I'm old fashioned that way."

Cassie smiled. "I'm old-fashioned, too. I like the idea of marriage. The permanency of it."

Becca slapped her forehead. "Oh shit! I forgot. I have a wedding present for you. Okay, not really a wedding present, more like a honeymoon present. I left it at my condo."

Cassie whistled. "Hot damn, a honeymoon present. I hope it's raunchy and debauched."

Becca headed for the door with a grin. "You can count on it. Be right back."

* * * *

"I think we made it clear to Becca that we want to be with her and that we don't miss being alone with each other."

Mark and Travis were headed back to their house after the rehearsal dinner. Mark wanted to talk to Travis about something serious.

Travis nodded. "I think she's convinced. She knows we love her. She just needed to hear that we love her as much as we love each other. She knows that now and can feel secure."

"I was thinking of another way that might make her feel secure."

Travis held up his hand. "I know what you're going to say. It's too soon to ask her to marry us. We can't rush her. This is a serious thing, and we need to give her serious time."

Mark exhaled impatiently. "How much time will be enough? We love her and she loves us. We already talk about the future. Forever. Why are we waiting to be happy? Will she be more sure in a month or two? Will you?"

"This isn't about me."

"Isn't it? You're the cautious one. Are you sure you don't want us to wait because you don't want change?"

"Fuck, no. I've been full speed ahead on this, and you know that. Shit, I was the first one to say 'I love you.'"

"Then why wait? Let's ask her tomorrow."

The silence in the car grew. Mark wasn't sure why Travis was hesitating if it wasn't his natural caution. Finally, Travis spoke.

"What if she says no?"

Mark reached over and grabbed Travis's hand. "Babe, she loves us. She'll say yes. You have to believe. I have to believe. She wants to be with us as much as we want to be with her. What do you say? We have the ring already. Let's ask her tomorrow. We can pull her aside during the reception and propose."

Mark could see Travis struggle and then relax. "Okay, let's go for it. We bought her a hell of a ring. If she hesitates, maybe the ring will put us over the top."

Mark laughed. "Way to think positive, babe."

Raindrops started to fall on the windshield. Mark reached in the backseat for the umbrella.

"Shit, Becca left her shoes for the wedding tomorrow in the backseat. We have to take them to her."

"Can't we take them tomorrow? I don't think the women are going to be too happy if we horn in on their girls' night."

"Aren't you just a little bit curious what the girls are doing tonight? What if they hired a stripper or something? Remember they went to see that *Magic Mike* movie."

Travis scowled and turned at the next corner. "We'll take the shoes tonight."

* * * *

Becca hummed an eighties tune as she pushed her front door open. She just needed to grab Cassie's gift, then she could get back to the festivities. They had decided to watch a double feature of *Flashdance* and *Footloose*.

She flipped on the light and froze as she saw something move out of the corner of her eye. She gasped in surprise and fear and tried to back out of the door, but his hand reached out and grabbed her arm and threw her on the couch, slamming the front door shut. She finally caught a glimpse of the intruder's face, and she knew who it was in an instant. Randall.

An extremely agitated Randall who was breathing hard, red faced, and brandishing a knife as he paced in the small space in front of her living room couch. One look around the room let her know he had been there for a little while before she showed up. Drapes were cut into shreds, along with the upholstery on her couch and chairs.

Anything that had been sitting on a flat surface was now strewn around the floor, and a can of spray paint sat on the end table. Apparently, she had interrupted him before he had a chance to deface her walls. Thank God for small favors.

Now she needed to calm him down, so she could talk her way out of here. She used her softest, calmest voice.

"Randall, you need to calm down and get out of here. You don't want to be here when my brother shows up. He's the sheriff, you know."

Randall stopped his pacing and scowled. "I know that. You and your family think you're so special. Always sticking your nose where it doesn't belong. I came here tonight to teach you a lesson about keeping out of things that don't involve you. You weren't supposed to be here! Now what am I supposed to do with you?"

The last words were almost yelled, and his face was an unbecoming shade of reddish purple.

"You need to leave. Just leave. My brother is on his way here, and you can't be here when he shows up."

Becca didn't feel bad about lying, but she was worried if too much time went by Jillian and Cassie would come looking for her. They didn't need all three of them being held at knifepoint.

Randall's eyes narrowed and his lips thinned, making him a lot less of a pretty boy than the first day she met him.

"Bullshit. Everyone is out getting ready for your sicko multiple wedding. What kind of slut marries two men?"

Becca wanted to point out it was probably better to be a slut than a criminal, but it didn't seem the right moment.

"Yes, he will be by. He's coming to pick up his fiancée. You need to get out of here right now. I'm his little sister. He'll kill you if he finds you here."

"Shut up! I need to think. I need to think about what I am going to do."

Randall started to pace back and forth again, muttering to himself and turning redder with every minute. Becca's gaze darted around the room looking for a weapon or a way to get his attention from her for just a second. She knew if she could just distract him, she could kick the knife out of his hands. This was just what she had been taught in self-defense class. Maybe if she got him talking, she could distract him.

"Was it you who vandalized my shop? And did you knock down the mailboxes here? Why did you knock them all down?"

Randall stopped and gave her an exasperated look. "Of course it was me. And I knocked down all the mailboxes because I didn't know which one was yours. I'm the one who was trying to spread rumors about your business, too. I wanted to teach you a lesson."

That explained Justin's words at The Party about not listening to anything bad about her.

"What did you hope to accomplish?"

"You were supposed to leave Addie alone. Do you know what my life is like? Do you have any idea? I've lost everything. I've lost my house, my business. I just needed a new start. But you had to interfere, didn't you?"

"It was Addie's money. You were trying to steal it away from her. That's wrong."

Randall's face twisted. "Addie didn't need all that money. I would have given it back when I got my business back, anyway. She was being stubborn about giving it to me. It will be mine anyway when she dies. What's wrong with getting some now?"

Becca barely controlled her anger. Randall was a coldhearted asshole who obviously didn't care about the well-being of a lovely old woman.

"It's wrong because it still belongs to her," she said with gritted teeth.

It was like arguing with a four-year-old.

"So, Randall, are you going to leave now? I think I've learned my lesson about interfering."

His eyes blazed with hatred. "Don't patronize me. I didn't come here to hurt you, but I can't just walk away now. You're going to have to come with me."

Becca's heart sped up at his pronouncement. As the sister of a sheriff, she knew the absolute worst thing she could do is let Randall take her anywhere. She had to fight tooth and nail to keep him here. Eventually, Cassie and Jillian would wonder what happened to her. She could only hope they wouldn't just barge in here and get themselves hurt.

Becca shook her head. "I'm not going anywhere with you."

Randall reached out to grab for her arm again, and she pulled back, angering him further. He grabbed for her again, pulling her to her feet and shoving her toward the door.

"Let's go. Now."

She tried to pull back as the front door opened and Mark and Travis came in with smiles on their faces.

"Hey, babe, what are you doing here? We thought you'd be at Cassie and Jillian's."

Randall's wide-eyed shock at their arrival was all she needed. She reared up and kicked his hand with all her strength, sending the knife skittering across the floor and into the kitchen. Mark and Travis reacted quickly to the unexpected situation. Mark smacked Randall in the face with the shopping bag he carried, and Travis took him the rest of the way to the ground, pressing his chest to the floor and bending his arms behind his back.

Mark pulled his phone out of his back pocket and called Ryan, while Travis gave her a smile.

"We leave you alone for one hour and this is what you get up to, huh? From now on, we don't let you out of our sight, woman. Nice karate kick, by the way. You told us you could kick butt, and you really can."

Becca smiled in relief. "I can, but it was nice to have the help. Good timing."

"We got your back, babe."

Mark hung up his phone. "Ryan's on his way here."

Becca hugged him. "I'm glad you're here, but I have to wonder why. What made you come here tonight?"

Mark held up the shopping bag. "You left your shoes for the wedding in the car. When we pulled up we were heading to Jillian and Cassie's place but saw your lights on and figured we'd try here first."

Becca gave a shaky laugh. "You used my shoes as a weapon? They better not be damaged, stud."

Jillian and Cassie walked through the open front door, and their mouths dropped open in amazement. Jillian looked at Travis, who was holding Randall on the floor.

"I'm afraid to ask what happened here. Cassie and I were getting worried, so we headed over here. We saw Mark and Travis's car. This sure is different than what we thought we would be walking into."

Becca laughed. She had a pretty good idea what they thought they would be interrupting.

"The man on the floor is Randall. He was trying to steal money from Addie. He was angry that we were able to stop him, so he vandalized the mailboxes, the shop, and here."

Jillian looked at him like he was navel lint. "You're an idiot. I can think of few criminals I defended that were dumber than you. You deserve to get caught."

Randall's face contorted with anger. "I would have gotten away with it if it wasn't for her."

Mark laughed. "Yeah, you would have gotten away with it, too, if it weren't for that dog and you meddling kids."

Becca couldn't hold in her laughter as sirens sounded in the distance. These men were perfect for her. Deputy Jason walked in a few minutes later and dragged Randall to his feet, slapping him in cuffs and hauling him off to his police car. Ryan showed up only moments after, with Jack, Zach, and Chase in tow, and took everyone's statement.

Ryan carefully placed the knife into an evidence bag with his handkerchief. "Good going, little sister, kicking this out of his hand. I'm glad you took your self-defense classes seriously. I'm proud of you."

Becca felt tears prick the backs of her eyes, and she launched herself at Ryan, giving him a big hug. "I don't think you've ever said you were proud of me before."

Ryan looked uncomfortable, seeking out Jillian's help. She just smiled indulgently.

"Of course I'm proud of you. What brother wouldn't be?"

Jack held out his arms for a hug. "I'm proud of you, too."

Becca gave him a bear hug before going back to her men. She felt very content standing between them.

Ryan handed the evidence off to Deputy Jason. "Well, I think that's it. We have a big day tomorrow, and we should all get some rest. Jillian, you're going home with Jack and me tonight. After this, I want you where we can keep an eye on you."

"But my girls' night—" Cassie protested.

Zach pulled her into his arms. "I agree with Ryan. I want our woman close. You can have your girls' night when we get back from our honeymoon. Tonight, Chase and I are staying with you."

Cassie pouted but gave in with good grace. Becca was pretty sure she wasn't all too upset about the turn of events.

Travis turned to her. "Let's get you home, babe. We could all use some sleep after tonight."

It was Becca's turn to pout. She whispered in his ear as he pulled her close, "Not too much sleep, I hope."

Chapter 17

Becca headed straight for the bedroom when they got back to Mark and Travis's house. Her adrenaline was still humming from earlier, and she couldn't wait to channel it into a night with her men. Travis leaned in the doorway looking good enough to eat and giving her an evil smile. He had the same idea she did.

"I think our woman is anxious to be loved, babe. She's practically naked already."

Becca had divested herself of everything but her bra and panties. She was already reclining in the middle of the bed. Mark gave her a smirk.

"She does seem pretty ready. You don't think they had a stripper at the girl's night, do you?"

A stripper? If only.

Becca laughed. "We talked about it, but there are no strippers to be had in Plenty. Poor us."

Travis walked over to the iPod dock. "That's where you're wrong, sweetheart. You just have to know where to look."

Dance music filled the bedroom, and Becca sucked in a breath as she realized what they had in mind.

Holy hot damn.

Travis and Mark started dancing to the music. Travis was such a liar. Mark had perfect rhythm, moving sensuously to the music. They started plucking open the buttons on their shirts, each one revealing more and more of their muscled chests. She bit her lower lip as their shirts were peeled off their yummy bodies and thrown to the side. Travis started a bump and grind, and she had to bite down on her knuckle to keep from crying out in excitement. Mark pulled him close, and she bit her hand harder as their bodies pressed close together as their mouths met. They brushed against each other to the music, their erections tenting their jeans when they pulled apart. It was all she could do not to hop off the bed and fall to their feet in worship. They were the sexiest men she had ever seen. And they were all hers.

Becca's panties were soaked with her honey and her nipples were tight with arousal as she watched them flick open the top buttons of their jeans and then start playing with the zippers. It seemed to take forever as they pulled them down one tooth at a time, pulled them up partway, then lowered them a little more. She had crawled to the end of the bed to get a closer look, and she reached out with greedy fingers to grab a handful of their jeans to pull them down. Mark quickly danced away with a grin, leaving her frustrated but even more turned on.

They both tugged their pants down at the same time, tossing them to the side, taking their socks with them. They were now only in boxer shorts, and she licked her lips in anticipation of their impressive cocks running over her tongue and filling her mouth. Mark pushed his boxer shorts off first, his dick already hard and throbbing. He danced to Travis and hooked his fingers in Travis's shorts, tugging them down inch by inch. Travis's cock sprung free, and Mark leaned down and gave it a playful lick. Becca's pussy clenched, wanting to be filled with their cocks. They were so beautiful. She needed them so much.

Mark finally slid Travis's shorts down his legs and tossed them right at Becca. She caught them with a giggle and gave them a triumphant twirl in the air. She fell back on the bed and applauded. It was the best show ever.

"Magic Mike's got nothing on you two. That was awesome. How can I show my appreciation?"

They stood in front of her, their cocks hard and ready. She reached out and stroked them base to tip, feeling the velvety texture and the steely hardness underneath. Her men groaned, and Mark tangled his fingers in her hair, tugging her head down. She knew what he wanted. She fell to her knees and began using her mouth and tongue to drive him wild.

"Aw fuck, baby. Your mouth is lethal. It feels so fucking good."

He pulled back with a groan, and his cock pulled out with a pop.

"I don't want to come yet. We want to come inside you. My turn in your ass tonight."

Becca felt almost dizzy at the prospect of her men loving her at the same time. It was an amazing feeling. One she hoped was repeated over and over for the rest of her life. She caressed their cocks.

"So, let's get this show on the road. I'm a desperate, horny woman who watched two of the sexiest men on the planet do a striptease. Have some mercy here. My panties are drenched."

Travis trailed his finger down the middle of her cleavage, sending a shiver of delight through her. He gave her a wicked smile, and before she knew what had happened, he had flicked open the closure on her bra.

"Take it off, baby."

Becca quickly shrugged out of her bra. "Isn't that my line? I should have had dollar bills for you guys tonight."

Travis's throaty chuckle sent her arousal higher. He pushed her back on the bed, and he and Mark pulled her panties down her legs and tossed them over his shoulder.

"We only take twenty-dollar bills."

"You're going to have to do more than strip for a twenty."

Mark's eyebrow quirked playfully. "What did you have in mind? Maybe this?"

Mark stretched out on one side of her and licked her nipple before sucking it into his mouth. Becca drew a sharp breath as more honey trickled out of her cunt. Travis lay down on her other side and began torturing her other nipple with his lips and tongue. Her nipples were directly connected to her clit, and their ministrations made her pussy and clit throb painfully. She needed a cock in her pussy. Now.

She pushed at their heads. "I need you to fuck me."

Mark started kissing a wet trail down her belly. "I'm not going to be rushed. I want to eat some of this pretty pussy. You're going to be begging us for cock before I'm done."

She knew how talented his mouth was. She knew she would be begging before long. Damn, if that wasn't what she wanted. She loved it just as much as they did when she was begging.

"But I am begging."

Travis shook his head. "Not yet. Not enough."

Mark pushed her thighs apart and nibbled his way up her inner thigh before pressing a finger deep into her wet pussy. She moaned as he pressed another inside her and began to finger fuck her, sending waves of pleasure through her abdomen. He bent his head and began to trace the folds of her cunt with his tongue, teasing her with light flicks on her clit. While Mark pleasured her pussy, Travis lavished attention on her breasts. His fingers and tongue played with the taut peaks, sending shots of pleasure straight to her clit and making her writhe on the bed so that Mark had to anchor her legs down.

"Please, please, please, let me come."

Becca was panting with arousal and need. Her men could give her more pleasure than she had ever dreamed of. Mark closed his mouth over her clit and let his teeth gently scrape the sides. She screamed their names as she fell over the edge, her orgasm shaking her with its intensity. They pleasured her until she couldn't take any more, begging for mercy. Her thighs were covered with her cream and her cunt was sensitive and swollen. Mark's tongue was light as a feather on her clit, giving it soft kisses until she groaned and pushed his head away.

He gave her a grin. "I don't hear much begging. If you want to be packed full of cock, you better get to it."

Becca had just spent the last five minutes begging for mercy from their hands and tongues. She gave them a disinterested shrug.

"I'm tired. Why don't we just climb into bed and get some sleep?"

Mark looked shocked, but Travis saw right through her.

"If you're tired, go ahead. Mark and I are going to stay up and have sex. You don't care, right?"

* * * *

Travis had to hide his laughter. Becca's horrified expression was too cute. She was backed into a corner and was now chewing her lip, trying to find a way out. Travis reached for Mark and fused their lips, their tongues rubbing against each other. Their swollen cocks were trapped between their bodies, the pre-cum smeared on their abdomens. Mark pulled away and pushed him down to lick and nip at his flat male nipples. Travis's cock seemed to swell even larger, and he ran his fingers through Mark's golden-blond hair, loving the silky feeling. He turned, and Becca was watching them with lust-filled eyes. What had started out as a joke was turning their pretty girl on. Her skin was flushed a pretty pink and her chest rose and fell with her shallow breaths.

"God, I love watching you two love each other."

Travis levered himself up and pulled her close for a kiss.

"We're glad. But the plan was for us to all be together tonight. Mark and I were just joking about you going to sleep. You were joking, weren't you?"

Becca giggled and trailed her fingers delicately down his torso to encircle his cock. He sucked in a breath as her hand rubbed him up and down but not quite as hard as he needed it. She was such a tease.

"I was joking. But Mark wanted me to beg more, so I wanted him to beg, too."

Mark laughed, his blue eyes sparkling. "You want me to beg, sweetheart? I'll beg. Can I fuck your ass, pretty please, with sugar on top?"

Becca gave an exaggerated sigh.

"Oh, I guess so."

Travis stretched out on the bed and beckoned to the woman he loved. "Then come here, pretty girl. Grab a condom from the nightstand and let's get this party started."

Becca grabbed the condom and made a show of suiting him up. She kissed his stomach and caressed his balls while she slowly rolled the condom down his already-straining cock.

"Fuck, woman. What are you doing to me?"

Becca licked up his stomach before giving him a gentle bite on his shoulder. Mark laughed and smacked her bottom, making her yelp.

"She's a biter, babe. She's bit my ass and chest and now your shoulder. If we don't watch her, she'll be biting our cocks."

Travis's cock jumped at the image. Anything Becca did to him would feel good. She finally took mercy on him and began lowering herself onto his dick. He groaned as her tight pussy swallowed his cock. It felt like the very best heaven and the most tortuous hell.

"There's nothing like sinking into your hot pussy, babe. Nothing."

* * * *

Nothing felt as good as her men's cocks inside her, either. Travis's steel-hard dick filled every nook and cranny of her pussy and was already moving her toward orgasm. She took a deep breath as she took the last inches of his cock. Her hands were anchored to his muscular chest, and she looked down into his soft brown eyes, almost golden with passion and love. Yes, definitely love. She was loved by these two wonderful men. She started to move, but Mark's hand stayed her.

"Not yet. Lie down on Trav's chest and relax for me. We're all going to do this together."

Becca settled herself on Travis's chest. She could feel his heartbeat strong underneath her. She moaned in delight as his fingers began to play with her nipples. She squirmed on top of him, earning herself another smack on the bottom from Mark.

"Stay still. I don't want to have to spank you."

Becca's cunt clenched. She loved her punishments.

"Fuck, Mark. Her pussy just about strangled my cock when you threatened to spank her. She wants it bad, babe."

Mark's warm hand rubbed her ass cheek. "You want it, baby? I'm the man to give it to you."

She barely had time to prepare herself before Mark's hand came down on her ass hard. The heat bloomed from her ass to her pussy and clit. She moaned and writhed on top of Travis's cock as Mark kept up the rhythm of two smacks on one ass cheek, then he moved to the other, then moved back. She ground herself against Travis, and his hands tightened on her shoulders. Mark smacked her low on the ass, getting part of her pussy, and it was all she needed. She screamed her climax as he continued to rain blows on her ass. Her whole body tightened, and the waves of pleasure seemed connected to the timing of the spanking. Mark's hand became softer and softer as she came down from her high, finally just rubbing her sore, hot cheeks. She gasped to catch her breath, amazed that Travis was still hard inside her. She pushed herself up on his chest.

"You didn't come, too?"

Travis shook his head. The strain on his face was clear. "I gritted my teeth and thought about the bar exam."

Becca collapsed back on his chest. "Holy hell. That was amazing."

She felt the cold dribble of lube in her ass crack and then Mark's fingers at her back hole.

"It's about to get more amazing, pretty girl. Just relax for me."

She consciously tried to relax as one, then two fingers worked her ass, stretching her for his cock. When he added a third, she felt the stretch and the burn, which rapidly turned to pleasure. Mark was right. This was amazing.

She panted with pleasure. "Oh! Mark, I need…I need…"

Mark ran a reassuring hand up and down her back. "I know what you need. You need a cock, don't you, sweetheart?"

"Yes, please. Please!"

She was aware that Travis was tense underneath her. His jaw was tight, and she knew it was his amazing self-control that held him back. He had to have felt Mark's fingers in her ass on his cock. He was holding back for her.

She felt Mark line up his cock, and then the blunt tip of his cock pressed at her ass. At first the muscles resisted, but the stretching had done the job. The tight ring gave way, and she felt the burn and the bite of pain before it morphed into incredible pleasure. Mark worked his cock in and out until finally she had taken every inch he had to give. Her body was quivering with pleasure, and she moaned their names in encouragement.

"Okay, baby, we're going to fuck you so good. Brace yourself against me."

Mark's voice sounded strained as he pulled her up so she was leaning back on his chest. Their bodies were covered with a fine sheen of sweat and the smell of sex hung in the air. She was completely stuffed full of cock, and the feeling made her light-headed and tingly.

Travis was the first to move. He pulled out and pressed back in as Mark pulled out. Travis pulled out as Mark thrust in. They kept this pattern, giving her the hard fucking she loved so much. There wasn't a moment she wasn't impaled on her men's cocks. Each thrust sent pleasure running like water through her veins. The heat of her arousal grew hotter as the men built up speed. Time stood still as they fucked her hard and faster, their breaths coming in grunts. She was on the edge of climax. Mark reached around and played with her clit.

Her reaction was instantaneous. She screamed as the orgasm hit her like a freight train. Pleasure so intense it was almost too painful to bear wracked her body. Her cunt and ass clamped down on their cocks. She rode the waves of pleasure until she was wrung out and exhausted, her body slumped on Travis's chest. They lay there catching their breath and enjoying the feeling of being as one. Finally, Mark started to move. She protested, but he kissed her damp neck with a regretful sigh.

"Sorry, sweetheart. We need to take care of the condoms. We'll be right back."

Mark pulled out of her sore ass carefully, and then Travis pulled from her cunt. She was half-asleep on the bed when they returned with a warm cloth to clean her up. They were sticky from her honey and sweat. After she was clean, they cuddled with her, one on each side, just the way she liked it. She always felt so loved and protected when her men surrounded her. Travis's hand stroked her bare back.

"Sleep, baby. We have a big day tomorrow."

Her men fell asleep quickly, their soft snoring making her smile. She loved sleeping between her men. Tomorrow was a big day, and not just for Cassie, Zach, and Chase. It was going to be a big day for her and her men, too.

Chapter 18

Mark was nervous. He and Travis were going to ask Becca to marry them today, sometime during the reception. Despite his bravado with Travis the night before, he, too, was worried Becca might say no. She was younger than they were, and perhaps she wasn't anxious to tie herself down. He knew she loved them. Her love shone out of her with every look and touch. But would it be enough for her to commit to them for a lifetime?

Travis squeezed his shoulder. "Relax. All we can do is tell her how we feel. If she says no, then we'll regroup and figure out plan B."

They were in Zach and Chase's backyard waiting for the wedding to start. Even Mark could appreciate the care that had gone into the wedding. The wedding was going to be held in the shade of some beautiful, old oak trees. Row upon row of white folding chairs had been set up for the guests, and the altar was decorated with an arbor of flowers.

A large tent had been erected just a few feet away with a dance floor, tables and chairs, a buffet, and an amazing six-tier wedding cake. Next to the wedding cake was a smaller chocolate groom's cake, as was the tradition in the South. It would be any girl's dream wedding.

"I want Becca to have a wedding like this, Trav. She deserves the whole thing."

Travis smiled. "She can have anything she wants. I just want her to be happy. Personally, I would be happy with a justice of the peace, but we'll do what she wants. I could get into a big shindig if she wants it."

"Jillian says Becca will want a wedding with her family there."

"You told Jillian we were going to propose today?" Travis sounded surprised.

"No, that's our business. I wouldn't have told her without letting you know. But she was talking about Becca and our future. She knows we want to marry her. We haven't exactly been hiding our feelings."

Travis laughed. "That's true."

Music started up, and people started to take their seats.

"Let's go sit down. The wedding is about to start."

Mark and Travis settled in their seats and turned to watch as Becca started gliding down the aisle. She looked gorgeous in a strapless blue dress that showed off her mouthwatering curves. Mark gave Travis a grin. That was their woman looking so luscious. They would be the envy of every man today. Jillian was next, and Mark gave his little sister an encouraging smile. Jillian preferred jeans and T-shirts to wedding finery, but she looked beautiful today. She favored their father but was pretty and delicate like their mother. Ryan and Jack were lucky men.

When the wedding march started, everyone stood up as Cassie floated down the aisle with a dreamy smile. Zach and Chase had the same smiles. Mark felt a pang of envy that it wasn't his wedding day.

He couldn't help a grin as he remembered Cassie when she was nothing but a child. She had been a skinny, flat-chested girl who favored books over playing outside. She had certainly blossomed into a beautiful woman. She looked like the princess she was today. Becca had styled Cassie's hair into a cascade of curls that fell down her back. Zach and Chase looked hypnotized by her beauty.

Cassie handed her flowers to Jillian, and Zach and Chase each took one of her hands. In a strong voice Zach promised to love, honor, and cherish his bride. No one could doubt the commitment Zach felt, hearing the certainty in his voice. Mark marveled at Chase's emotion-filled voice as he, too, promised to love, honor, and cherish Cassie.

Chase could be teasing and charming, but today he was obviously overcome with emotion. Cassie's voice was soft and sure. She repeated her vows twice—once to Zach and once to Chase. Mark felt a lump form in his throat as he pictured the three of them standing under a flower-covered arbor vowing to love one another until death.

By the time they were pronounced men and wife, Mark was fighting the tears. Travis put his arm around him and whispered in his ear, "Remember when we said those words to each other that day in Hawaii? I felt married to you even before then, but when we said them that day, it was like a vow in my heart."

Mark held Travis's hand tightly and nodded. "I love you, Trav."

"I love you, too, babe. Let's make Becca part of our family, okay?"

"Okay, let's do it."

* * * *

Cassie was sipping at her orange juice and taking her last bite of wedding cake. It had been a beautiful wedding. Cassie was dancing with Zach, her smile dazzling at her new husband. She looked amazing in her traditional white satin wedding gown. It was off the shoulder with a tight beaded bodice and ball-gown skirt made with tiers of tulle. It was a dress for a dream wedding, and that's what this had been. The only thing to mar the day was Cassie's estranged family hadn't come for the wedding. Cassie hadn't been all that surprised, as they disapproved of her relationship with two men, but Mike, Steve, and Ellie had stepped in and tried to play parents of the bride for her.

"C'mon, pretty girl. Let's go for a little walk."

Travis was holding out his hand with a smile. She didn't hesitate to put her hand in his. Mark grabbed her other hand, and she let them lead her off from the party. They finally stopped in the shade of a tree, and they motioned for her to sit down on a fallen log. They stayed standing and seemed to pace back and forth. Mark ran a finger around his neckline as if his tie was too tight.

"Um, are you guys all right?"

They came to a halt in front of her with nervous smiles. They were up to something.

Travis lifted her fingers to his lips. "Becca, we love you."

"I love you, too."

"And we've waited a long time for you."

"I've waited for you, too."

Mark sat down next to her. "What Travis is trying to say is, this is everything we ever dreamed of."

"Me, too."

The men exchanged a glance, and then both went down on one knee. Becca felt a little dizzy and forced herself to breathe.

Mark held her hand. "Becca, no one could love you more than we do. We're better with you than without you. Will you marry us?"

Travis held her hand in both of his, his voice urgent. "We will love and protect you forever. Will you marry us?"

Becca blinked back tears. She had given up on finding this kind of love for herself, and now it was here and being offered to her for a lifetime. She nodded her head vigorously, a lump making speech difficult.

"Yes! Oh, yes! I want to marry you."

They were hugging and kissing her for the longest time. She finally laughed and pulled free.

"Well, I'm really glad you want to marry me. Do you want kids, too?"

Their faces split into grins. Mark leaned forward and gave her another kiss.

"We would love to have kids. We don't want to pressure you, though. If you want to wait a while, we're fine with that."

Becca shook her head. "I'm glad you want kids, because I have some news."

She paused, trying to find the right words.

"Well, the thing is, I'm kind of surprised myself. I took the test a few days ago when this crazy nausea wouldn't go away. Boys, I'm pregnant."

Shock was the only way to describe their expressions, which quickly gave way to delight. She breathed a sigh of relief. She hadn't been sure how they would take the news. To be honest, she was still a little shocked herself.

Mark ran a hand down his face. "Holy shit, a baby. Are you sure, honey?"

Becca rolled her eyes. "You're a doctor, Mark. Do you need to see the blue stick?"

Mark groaned and pulled her close. "I guess I've always been better with empirical evidence. But it does all make sense now. We've made love for five weeks straight with no break. Plus the fact you haven't been feeling like yourself. We're going to have a baby!"

Travis pulled her from Mark's arms. "Hey, let me get in here, too. Sweetheart, this is wonderful news. Surprising, but wonderful. We used a condom every time."

Becca nodded. "I know. One must have leaked or something. I wasn't on the pill or anything. I guess we should have been more careful."

Travis laughed. "With you, baby, my cautious nature goes right out the window. More careful? Hell, no, we're going to be parents."

Becca smiled. "I wasn't sure how you were going to take the news. I'd planned to tell you tonight. I didn't want to steal any of Cassie's thunder today."

Both Mark and Travis nodded in agreement. Mark pulled her to her feet and pulled a square box out of his jacket pocket. He flipped it open, and she sucked in a breath as the most beautiful ring lay nestled in the blue satin. It was a square-cut diamond that flashed fire in a platinum setting. The band was encrusted with diamonds that sparkled in the sunlight.

"Holy shit, this must have cost a fortune."

Mark and Travis slid the ring on her finger. Travis lifted her hand and kissed her ring finger.

"Nothing is too good for our woman. If you don't like it, we can exchange it."

"No way. I love it. I love you! Both of you."

Mark pulled her close. "All we're asking for is forever. That's not too much, is it?"

Becca shook her head and wiped a tear from her cheek.

"I think forever sounds just right."

Mark gave her a smile and grabbed Travis's hand.

"Rebecca Parks, I promise to love, honor, and cherish you from this day forward, until death do us part. You and Travis are my life, my heart, and my future. I promise to be the best husband and father I possibly can. I promise to make you feel special every day of your life."

Travis held her hand tightly in his. "Rebecca Parks, I promise to love, honor, and cherish you from this day forward, until death do us part. You and Mark are my life, my heart, and my future. I promise to make our family a haven of love, happiness, and comfort. I promise to show you both I love you each and every day God blesses us with."

Becca felt the tears fall down her cheeks but ignored them. She was too caught up in this moment with the men she loved. She held their hands close to her heart and swallowed the lump in her throat.

"Mark Miller and Travis Andrews, I promise to love, honor, and cherish you from this day forward, until death do us part. Both of you, and our child, are my life, my heart, and my future. I promise to spend the rest of my life showing you how much I love each of you and never take a day of our life together for granted."

Travis smiled, his brown eyes shining with love. "I now pronounce us husband—"

"Another husband, and wife," finished Mark.

Becca smiled through her happy tears. "You may now kiss the bride."

And they did for quite a while.

THE END

WWW.LARAVALENTINE.NET

ABOUT THE AUTHOR

I've been a dreamer my entire life. So, it was only natural to start writing down some of those stories that I have been dreaming about.

Being the hopeless romantic that I am, I fall in love with all of my characters. They are perfectly imperfect, with the hopes, dreams, desires, and flaws that we all have. I want them to overcome obstacles and fear to get to their happily ever afters. We all should. Everyone deserves their very own sexy happily ever after.

I grew up in the cold but beautiful plains of Illinois. I now live in Central Florida with my handsome husband, who's a real native Floridian, and my son, whom I have dubbed "Louis the Sun King." They claim to be supportive of all the time I spend on my laptop, but they may simply be resigned to my need to write.

When I am not working at my conservative day job or writing furiously, I enjoy relaxing with my family or curling up with a good book.

For all titles by Lara Valentine, please visit
www.bookstrand.com/lara-valentine

Siren Publishing, Inc.
www.SirenPublishing.com

CPSIA information can be obtained at www.ICGtesting.com
Printed in the USA
LVOW04s1658140615

442438LV00022B/773/P